THE VOID

A NOVEL

Alain Lea

Foreword by Steve McVey, Bestselling Author of "Grace Walk"

If you only read the books everyone read or will read, you will eventually think just like everyone. This is the difference – it is that good!

PRAISES FOR THE VOID

In *The Void*, Alain Lea has touched the fundamental nerve within the human heart – the need and desire to believe that we matter. There is a thirst to know that our lives serve a greater purpose than to drink from the shallow waters of pleasure, position and possessions until the clock runs out and the game is over in this world.

The Void gave a clear understanding of the nature and character of God. You will never be the same again after reading this book. Make sure you give someone else the opportunity to be transformed through it as well.

Dr. Steve McVey
President of Grace Walk Ministries
Best-Selling Author

The Void is a heart grabbing story of a relentless friend who chooses to share a life changing truth he has found with the friends he loves. This novel reminds me of the passionate pursuit Jesus is on and is doing with all humanity. Each person is being personally pursued by the loving Pursuer, who has determined that not one will outrun, outlast or outdo His loving patient pursuit. This novel is fascinating and gripping and its ending will leave you begging for more. Well done Alain.

Kyle Butler
Pastor/Teacher/Motivational Speaker
New Jersey USA

§

The Void is an honest look at how Christianity is portrayed through the eyes of people today, especially the youth. From one side you have one who knows God through grace and relationship and the other's view through disappointments in life. See how the forces of Light collide with the powers of darkness; how religion meets reality. Indeed inspiring.

Hector Rivas
Tunisia

§

After reading *The Void*, I could not think of God differently than the Lover of the human race. This book completely challenges the theology of today and provokes a profound reflection on the nature and character of God. I am impressed by the gospel that my beloved brother shares here. It is powerful and really satisfying for the soul of the reader. I invite the youth but also the adults to read this book and receive the thought of God in Jesus Christ our Savior. Don't hesitate to give it away as a gift to those you love and care about.

Pastor Rémy BAYLE

President & Founder of Fire and Glory Ministry (France)

This book is a timeless literary gift that will leave an indelible impact upon every reader. If you have experienced relational brokenness, disillusionment, and disappointment in the pursuit of love, then The Void was written just for you. It presents the extravagant love of GOD in a relevant presentation that will transform your life and re-calibrate the trajectory of your destiny.

Pastor Gregory R. Morris

Associate Pastor at Freedom Church - Chicago, Illinois (USA)

§

When I was reading *The Void*, I was going through an extremely difficult transition in my personal life. This story has blown the door wide open to my soul and the ones of my kids. I can't be grateful enough for what *The Void* did in my house. If you read one work of fiction in this season, let it be this one.

Dr. Juana P. Wilson
Doctor and Business Owner – Oslo, Norway

§

Timely book in this season of rapid reform and awakening of the church of Christ. *The Void* is a one-of-a-kind invitation to a journey into the very heart of God. Through my tears and cheers, I have been indeed changed and transformed by the tender mercy with which Alain Lea opened the veil that too often separates man from the loving and true God. I rate each of these pages 100 out of 10. This novel is a series to enjoy. I can't wait to get my copy of Volume 2. This is a MUST-READ, dear beloved, in this generation and the one to come.

Miss. Juanita Heydenreich
International Distributor of Engineering Product
Emalahleni, South Africa

§

Sweat, wonder, transparency and surprises are the words I can use to define this book after reading through it. It feels like being set free from a very heavy burden from page to page. I will say, this work of fiction blew the door of my soul wide open.

Prophetess Chimwemwe V.K. Nyirenda
Beauty and Glory of God

ISBN: 978-1-952806-00-1 (paperback)
ISBN: 978-1-952806-01-8 (eBook)
ISBN: 978-1-952806-02-5 (hardback)
ISBN: 978-1-952806-03-2 (audio)

Christ In All Nations, Inc

info@christinallnations.org
P.O Box: 588
Granger, IN 46530
www.christinallnations.org

Cover design and page layout by HCP Book Publishing.

Printed in the United States of America

This book is dedicated to everyone who presently feels or has felt empty on the inside; to everyone who God loves, which is all of mankind.

Jesus mirrors our completeness and endorses our true identity.

TABLE OF CONTENTS

ACKNOWLEDGMENTS

Thank you, Abba Papa, for being everything to me: for me, in me and with me. You began by unveiling sonship in me, freeing me to announce the same sonship in all men. I celebrate Your life in me.

Special thank you to Paul, John and all those who remained faithful in defending the traditional knowledge of Father, Son and Holy Spirit. Today, our generation, just like many before mine, can behold the beauty of our God and Father as in the mirror through the face of the dear and eternal Son of the Father.

Writing a book is harder than I thought and more rewarding than I could have ever imagined. None of this would have been possible without the awesome family God blessed me with. From reading early drafts, to giving me advice on the cover, to keeping the munchkins out of my hair so I could edit; each one of them was as important to this book getting done as I was. Your enthusiasm each time I was editing gave me all I needed to share this masterpiece with a wider audience, in print, audio and, hopefully, in film. Thank you so much.

Thank you to Apostle Beth Thomas and Sister Amy Rice, for working day and night with me to bring this story to its final form, adding your insights into keeping the story true to Christian's pain, love, compassion, kindness, and perseverance toward his friends' experience of Christ as their only Life. You guys brought energy, creativity, and skill to this writing. The quality of work that people now hold in their hands is due to your sacrifice and gifts. Thanks a lot!

Thanks to all who intersected this project and gave your time and heart to polish the surface, to voice an opinion or speak an encouraging word. You left a piece of yourself in this story and how it has unfolded. These include Susannah Philips (UK), Rachid (Pakistan), Doumbe Endene Marie (CMR), Marcus Thomas (USA), Moses Thomas (USA), Jordan Alvarado (USA), Anne Kiunga (USA), Shadrack Mibeere (USA), Joe Alvarado (USA), Chantal Reymond (Swiss), Pastor Boniface Odhiambo (Kenya), Remy Bayle (France), and Epossi Monique (CMR).

I want to especially thank every individual who willingly offered their lives to share the true nature of God around the world. Thanks for revealing to all men their original design, worth and authentic identity in God. What makes it even better are people who share the gift of their time to mentor youth in the ways of God.

Thank you to everyone who strived to grow and help others grow in this extravagant understanding of the pure and unchanging love of God and Father of our Lord Jesus Christ. God is not in the business of excluding man but including by saving what He Himself created in His image and likeness. I usually say it this way, "Mankind was invited before the worlds began to mutually indwell in God, in Eternity."

To all the gifted individuals I have had the opportunity to be led by or watch their leadership from afar, I want to say a special thank you. Thanks to Dr. Shawn and Annie Smith, founders of Gospel of Christ Ministries and Author of "Compendium of Paul's Epistles;" Steven McVey, founder of Grace Walk Ministries and Author of "Grace Walk;" Dr. C. Baxter Kruger, Director of Perichoresis and Author of "The Great Dance;" WM. Paul Young, Author of "the Shack;" Kay Fairchild, founder of New Life Ministries and Author of "Living Out of Your Spiritual Resources;" and Francois Du Toit, Author of "Mirror Bible." You have all been the inspiration and foundation for what I do today.

Without the experiences and support from my peers and the team at Christ In All Nations Inc, this book would not exist. You have given me the opportunity to lead a great group of individuals—to be a leader of great leaders is a blessed place to be. Thank you to Beth, Mark, Joe, Anne, and Shadrack, to name a few.

Having an idea and turning it into a book is as hard as it sounds. The experience is both internally challenging and rewarding. I especially want to thank my precious and lovely mother, Doumbe Endene Marie, for her great leadership and constant support in everything I do.

Complete thanks to Pastor Bernard Berlin Modo; you believed in me when I did not know anything about God. You trusted me with people I could share the word of Christ with.

Rev. Dr. Shawn Smith, thank you for being a leader I trust, honor, and respect. I will always welcome the chance to listen to what the Father of our Lord Jesus Christ placed in your heart.

FROM THE AUTHOR

The world, seen through Jesus Christ our Savior, is a beautiful place. Unfortunately, most of us are unable to see in that manner because we get lost struggling with temptations that employ lust to lure us into a trap. Just like what happens in hunting and fishing, we are deceived by attractive baits, of which our desires could be a part of. Thank God for His goodness and affection revealed through Jesus Christ. He has no intention to condemn anyone. He sent his Son, not to be the judge, but the Savior of the world. So, this is an invitation to see and realize that salvation has already been provided for everyone; but each individual should experience it. Let us enjoy God's embrace and care as His Spirit takes us through the path He prepared for us.

Jesus loves you, just as much as He loves me. He died the death we deserved in order for us to realize the extremity of His unconditional love for us. We were bankrupt in our efforts to save ourselves, but Jesus showed up on our behalf. So, salvation is not a reward for good behavior. It has absolutely nothing to do with what we have done. God's mercy, through Christ Jesus, saved us.

This novel is an invitation to find deep within us the transcendental love of our Savior. Through the adventures of a group of young people, who could very well be you or your children or even grandchildren; see how God's Word and Wisdom is triggered into action when we cease our own efforts to justify ourselves by yielding to the message of Christ. His Word penetrates and impacts their lives in such a way that they live the blessed life that Jesus gives them, while the Void in their hearts and minds disappear.

This novel is also for those who want to know why they were born on this planet. You must begin with God to answer that question. You were born by and for His purpose. This novel takes that truth and gives it flesh for the sake of allowing the best of God's masterpiece to be displayed through your life.

This novel will help you see how horrible it is to go through moments of feeling the void, emptiness, sadness, despair, rejection, sorrow, unfulfillment, not enough, unhappiness and misery. Whatever situation you are in right now, the journey you are embarking on through this book will open your eyes like never before and challenge what you have known about God and about yourself. You will encounter Jesus himself in your soul in an unusual way.

The Void can make one do things that one would end up regretting. When one feels incomplete, there is not much joy left in life because one is always striving to make ends meet and feel better. The Void makes one run after shallow pleasures and sinful thoughts. Jesus' immediate presence is closer to you than any sense you could ever have of His absence. Ask the disciples in the eye of the storm, in the middle of the ocean, scared beyond their wits until they heard, *"Ego eimi"* which is translated, "I am." You have no reason to fear. Jesus is not away from you but right inside you.

The love of God will overflow your heart with a feeling of happiness and joy. It is infinite and it is for everyone. Kindly be open while reading this story and invite Him to live His life in and through you. Everything beautiful about life and every little miracle we encounter in our path is the result of His finished work.

It is true that life can be tough at times. We can experience loss, temptation, roughness and a million other things, but it is under His guidance that those moments can be dealt with without falling into depression, addiction, or any other harmful practice.

For a believer, the life of Christ is not an addition to His life. Instead, it is the only life there is, so he lives it to the fullest potential.

Jesus wants you to know that you have been included in the relationship of the ages. He wants to hear from you and show you everything that belongs to you. He loves you so much and simply wants you to know that. He does not want you to miss the enjoyment which is in the relationship He has made you a partaker of. You do not need to sacrifice anything to earn what He freely made available for you in Him. All you need to do is simply believe that the work of Jesus Christ was for you; He took your sins away and redeemed His beauty in you. His death was the death of the cosmos; God raised Him to life and now He lives forever, which is the guarantee of your eternal life. The life, death, resurrection, ascension, and seating of Jesus Christ was vicarious, meaning, all that happened to him equally happened to all men.

Live a life of thanksgiving and rejoice always for He has given you His all. He does not want anything in return for His gift of salvation. What He desires is that, by faith, every man comes into the knowledge of this reality, which has been made available to mankind through Christ Jesus. Once you awaken to the knowledge of His opinion about you, there will be no more Void to be filled, no more feeling of emptiness or sadness. In everything, we have been made more than conquerors through Him who loved us.

This novel is an invitation to rest. Again and again in the Scriptures, men and women are graciously invited to participate in a personal fellowship with God. As you go through this novel, you will realize that you are saved, by grace through faith in Jesus Christ. You are engineered by God's design. He modeled and manufactured you in Christ. He has plans for you; the ultimate, which is your eternal participation in the shared life of Father, Son, and Holy Spirit.

As a minister of the Gospel of Jesus Christ who travels and preaches all over the world, I come across a lot of people with different stories from every walk of life. There are some things that touch me deeply about the people God puts in my path. Firstly, He loves them more than words will ever express. If I could get each person I encounter to grasp this fact, then no one would be lost in their own darkness. Alas, we live in a world where the system established by men breaks people. Secondly, each person has a unique story that can help others. Every experience and lesson learned is valuable and has the ability to change lives. Thirdly, each person I meet has value and deserves dignity.

I only have one chance when I am traveling, unless there are multiple nights I am preaching, and that never seems to be enough. I wrote this novel to reach the young people I see often, but never have enough time to talk with. Life has a way of hurting them so they will be immobilized and ineffective. The totalitarian lie is one of the most destructive ones our generation believes in today. Why? Totalitarians control thoughts and actions by controlling speech. They deny that human nature has limits. They believe humans create reality. But Christians, especially, should be able to recognize the ideas of those who envision a world without God—and we cannot forget what some have done in their pursuit of it. Satan is, after all, both a murderer and the father of lies. Today, young people believe that if you stumble, you should stay down. That is not true.

I want our young people to know that no matter what they have done, redemption has been made available for them by grace, through faith in the life and the sacrifice that Jesus Christ made on the cross. Ultimately, there are many ways to get off track: drugs, alcohol, sex, other addictions, bad decisions, crime, gang involvement, lying, stealing, murdering - the list is longer than I want to drag on with. We don´t need to try hard or force ourselves to perform any task to cause an impression or chase happiness. If we abide in Him and His words abide in us, we will experience His best throughout our lives in this generation and the one to come. The God and Father of our Lord Jesus Christ loved you, loves you and will *always love you.* He knows the mistakes you have made, and He loves you regardless.

This is the story of eight friends. Some might be relatable to you as you read. They struggle and make fun of a guy named Christian, a devoted and lover of Jesus. These guys have issues and you will see their pain, their anger, their changes, or its absence, in some instances.

We all have things holding us back: poverty, anger, our background, socioeconomic standing, educational barriers; this is another list that can run on and on. I am here to tell you that those barriers were rendered obsolete at the cross – remember, Jesus said, ***"It is finished."***

So, I am happy to entice all kinds of people to read this novel.

To everyone who is yet to finally experience salvation in Christ, I want you to know that life makes a whole lot of sense when we live, move and rest in the love of God. Do not overlook it.

As you are holding this special book right now, I pray that as you read it, you will experience the living Christ in you and a permanent presence of His Holy Spirit with you wherever you are. Get ready for this adventure. Enjoy the book, and I will see you again at the end.

My prayers are for you as you read. It will be fun from
beginning to end.

Apostle Alain Lea

CHAPTER ONE

Devin was covered from head to toe in black. His balaclava covered everything but his eyes, and he was sure he looked gangster with the sunglasses. They completed the look. He had been waiting some time to get into this outfit and it felt awesome to be wearing "war clothes."

Devin was up for a promotion. He had to show the gang leaders he could be trusted with more work and do it better than the guys under him. He had decided this was his life now, and it was not a light commitment – he knew he would be "jumped out" if he tried to leave. That was usually fatal, and he knew it. He was playing with fire, walking the thin red line that separated being alive in the gang food chain or dead. He understood that going in and he knew getting in had been easier for him than most. His father helped him with that – but once he was in, he made the gang a lot of money quick.

This new job meant twice as much, at least. It was a major league. But for Devin, it wasn't really about the money, it was about the loyalty. It was not long ago he betrayed a lifelong friend to prove he was giving up his old life for the gang.

Devin knew tonight was going to be tough and possibly dangerous, but he had been pumping himself up all day. He had taken some liquid courage to keep him going forward. He was anticipating this moment, talked to everyone in the gang, and listened to their stories to help prepare for what could be in store for him. From what he had heard, it was not going to be easy or simple. When the gang decided to test one of their own, they hit them where it hurt the most.

The President was going to be there. He planned to put Devin in charge of the prospects and a leader had to be tough and cruel for that. How can you order the beating or initiation of someone, if you can't take or dole out violence yourself? The President needed to know how far Devin was prepared to go for the gang.

Over the last few months, Devin had been getting into the ring with some of the toughest competitors for rank. He had been brutally beaten a few times, left unconscious from a kick to the head or fists to the face. As soon as he was back from his injuries, he had to go back to it. Instead of getting scared, Devin would pump some iron and challenge the competitor again and again until he had beaten him. He refused to lose, and the Boss liked that about him. A President with the street name 'Boss' - Devin wanted a cool name given to him too.

"You ready, kiddo?" Boss slid his own sunglasses on.

"Whenever you are." Devin answered firmly. He was confident in himself but the fact that there was only Boss and his next-in-line coming along made him nervous. This was meant for all the senior guys to go along with and he hadn't heard a story yet where they weren't all along for the show.

Boss climbed into the Cadillac and Big Dog, the next-in-line, slipped into the backseat. Devin stood outside the vehicle, confused. Boss leaned over from the driver's seat, "You getting in, man? You gettin' cold feet?"

"Nah, just don't want to show disrespect. Big Dog should be up here." Devin knew exactly what buttons to push to please his superiors.

"Nah, dog, you good. Thanks for checking though. Brownie points for sure." Big Dog nodded his approval.

Devin got in feeling pretty important sitting in the front with Boss. It was not something everyone experienced. Boss looked at him with a fierce expression. He had pearly teeth but a menacing grin. Devin was a little scared, but he was determined to pull it off and play it cool.

"If I'm going to put you in charge of soldiers, I need to know you're up to the task. Do you understand me?"

"Fo' sure. I get it. What are we doing?" Devin wanted to get this over with so he could relax, but he couldn't make it seem obvious that he wanted it done.

"Cool your jets, boy, we're talking to you for a minute. What was that kid's name that always pestered you about

Jesus? That one you called crazy?" Boss' smile seemed even more sinister and Devin's expression faltered a touch.

"Christian, yeah, that dude is a mess." It was funny they remembered the call from the other day though. He must be more important to them than he realized and the fact that they were paying close attention made him feel special.

"Ha, what a name for a Jesus freak." Big Dog hit the headrest of Devin's seat, laughing.

Devin laughed too. "I never even thought of that."

"Where does he live?"

"Over by the gas station."

"Cool." Boss looked at Big Dog and turned the car off the main street. Devin looked out the window and listened for any clue to what they were going to do tonight. Then he saw the gas station up ahead.

"Yo, Boss, we headed to Christian's?"

"Sure are. Damn, you're a fast one."

"…Yo' havin' me beat him up?" Devin felt a jump of trepidation inside, but Boss shook his head and Big Dog rumbled from the backseat, sounding pleased he thought about it.

"Nah, you ain't got to beat him up."

Boss pulled into an alley right beside Christian's foster parents' house, letting the engine idle. "You wanna be in charge of the prospects and have all the soldiers looking up to you, right?"

"Of course, that's why we're here."

Big Dog leaned between the seats. "You willing to do anything? Because there's no turning back now. You understand all that, right?" Devin turned to look at him, struck by how he looked tougher and ice cold up close.

"I get it, man. I get it. What do you need me to do?"

Boss and Big Dog exchanged a glance. "Put your hand out."

Devin started to put his gloved hand out, but Boss snapped, "Take your gloves off, dude. C'mon, you gotta know better. I need to see what you're made of."

Devin took his gloves off and Boss placed a 9mm into his hand. Devin blinked at it, his blood running cold and his chest suddenly tight. He finally asks, "What is this for?"

"You have your prints on it now bro, and it's loaded, don't forget it."

Devin didn't want to face what this was about, so he asked again, "I get it, what do I need to do?"

Big Dog's teeth showed through his balaclava and his menacing growl sent chills through Devin. "It ain't that hard, man. Go kill Christian. I'll be close behind you."

"You want me to go in and put a bullet in his head, and then we're gone? I dig, but how do I get in?"

"You gotta figure it out man, all of it." Boss sounded annoyed. He didn't like when someone lower hesitated. If he told someone to do something, they shouldn't need to ask questions or think about it. They should just act. He knew Devin got this and that he was just being insecure about the job he was given to do.

Devin got out of the car. His heart was thudding in his chest and his throat. He couldn't feel his fingers. He tried not to be seen by anyone as he made it to the back door and thought to check the doorknob. It turned.

Devin entered the house. There were nightlights all over the place because this was a safe home for foster children. It made it easier for Devin to find his way through the house. He hadn't been here overnight since a year or two after Christian came to live here and hoped Christian hadn't changed rooms in the house.

Devin walked slowly, looking everywhere. Adrenaline was flooding his system heightening every sense. He kept his pace steady and his mind still, refusing to think as he turned the corner and faced the hallway that would take him to Christian's room.

Christian's door was wide open. Devin was relieved to see his window was also open. The gun would be loud, and the window would make his escape easier. Christian's room was over the front porch and there was a trellis for the climbing flowers his foster mom grew at the front of the house.

Devin entered the room and gently closed the door, easing the gun from his waistband. No part of him could believe he was about to shoot Christian. A million thoughts and memories bombarded his mind as he stood at the foot of the bed, aiming at Christian with a loaded

9mm. *What will life be like after he pulled the trigger? Should he do it in the head, and make it quick? Or in the chest, off center, to give him a chance to survive?* His hand was shaking. He couldn't make up his mind. Everything was moving too fast for him to decide. The gun wavered in the air and he tried to swallow, but his throat was too thick and tight to let him. It was cold, he noticed. It was cold, and he didn't want to do this. This was *Christian*. His friend, the boy he had known for so long and shared his childhood with. He was pointing a gun at his *friend*.

He kicked the bed frame with his boot. Christian snapped awake. As soon as Devin was sure Christian could see him, he leveled the gun at him again.

Christian looked from the barrel of the gun to Devin's face. There was a long moment where neither of them moved, then Christian closed his eyes, visibly praying, "Love is large in being passionate about life and relentlessly patient in bearing the offenses and injuries of others with kindness. Love is completely content and strives for nothing. Love has no desires to make others feel inferior and has no need to sing its own praises. Love is predictable and does not behave out of character. Love is not ambitious. Love is not spiteful and gets no mileage out of another's mistakes. Love sees no joy in injustice. Love's delight is in everything that truth celebrates. Love is a fortress where everyone feels protected rather than exposed. Love's persuasion is persistent. Love believes.

Love never loses hope and always remains constant in contradiction."

After these words, Christian started to speak in unknown tongues, then, he whispered, "Go ahead. Please don't hurt anyone else."

Devin's head reeled. He didn't lower the gun but looked straight into his old friend's eyes. They were at complete peace. But his, he knew, were shiny and ready to pour a sea of angry tears. *Why wasn't Christian begging for his life?* The calmness, the acceptance – it undermined Devin's confidence, and took him places he didn't want to go. *How much inner peace did Christian really feel, if he didn't seem panicked at all?* He just asked that no one else suffered.

CHAPTER TWO

They say that when one faces their own mortality, their lives flash before their very eyes like snippets from a movie. Some of the scenes roll by in slow motion, while others are like a lucid dream. The mind doesn't get to choose where the scenes from life begins, or how it ends.

Christian's life was no different from any other boy or girl in the hood. They knew hard life, and everyone had a story to tell, and skeletons in their closets, but they all knew each other, and some were closer friends than others.

In Christian's circle, he had eight friends. They all knew each other from childhood, and grew up together, sharing many experiences together, until one day Christian made a choice that put him on the outside of his circle of friends, but he refused to walk away.

It was the summer holidays, maybe one or two years prior and a time for friends to hang out. Summer rolled in quicker this year than it usually does, as if time was encroaching on itself. Call it global warming or just the anticipation of getting away from the classroom and the intellectual badgering of the teachers, but summer was always welcomed. Christian watched as his friends from the neighborhood played basketball. He once played with them, but no more. No one picks him to play on their side anymore. Now the teams were even, four on four. That's how they wanted it anyway, but no one was ever willing to step down.

No one would suspect that these guys were even friends at school. They were an unlikely bunch; more different than they were alike, which resulted in many explosive fights, but here they were playing a team sport on the court.

The nine have been friends since kindergarten. They knew each other inside out and have seen the best and worst times in life, yet there was a bond from a shared background that knitted the friendship between these young men. Oh, there is one girl, but she's a tomboy so everyone sees her as one of the guys. Her name is Mitch, so if she doesn't reveal her gender, you would never know. There were differences in persona; pretty big and noticeable differences, each to his own, but usually after hours of shooting hoops, these guys would settle down and talk about life, but things were a little different now. Christian was somehow relegated to the outcasts department because of that life-transforming decision he made. He had a harsh beginning too but felt like he needed something to fill the teenage void within, and he found it in the most unlikely place; he found a cure for excessive worry and unhappiness; a buffer for personal problems. It came at a cost. He was now separated from his friends. There was the eight, and then there was Christian.

As they chased each other up and down the court, Will started joking with Colton, "Did you find it yet?"

Colton was obviously annoyed. He liked to focus on his game because he wanted to play varsity this upcoming year, and the competition was steep, "Find what?"

Will flashed a grin in Christian's direction, always talking loud enough for him to hear, "You know what I'm talkin' about! Something to fill the big emptiness…that void," Will pointed at his heart and pretended to be sad.

Christian was familiar with their conversations. They thought he had changed too much and too quickly. When he tried to tell them about the source of his change, they wouldn't hear it. They cared very little for his newfound religious persuasion. They wanted to live life on their own terms, but Christian knew the void he felt all those years was in them as well. It was in every single human being. It was that emptiness that we try to fill with everything but the only *one* who can fill it. Christian found something that humanity was trying so hard to find and have. He resolved in his heart that his friends could make all the fun they wanted to make, but one day the choice would be theirs to make, just as it was his. The day comes for all to make the choice and Christian would never give up on his friends.

Will sashayed over and took his usual seat, wiping sweat from his brow.

"Hey, Christian, don't you get tired of sitting on the sidelines," He asked.

"You guys won't let me play."

"They will, if you just shut up with all that religious mumbo jumbo."

Will was a loner. His parents worked around the clock to make ends meet. Movies and television shows had become his babysitter and Christian didn't help much with always trying to get under his skin.

"I had another dream last night."

Will rolled his eyes, "Oh, seriously, dude. Just stop."

"You feel the void inside you, don't you, Will, the emptiness?"

"The only emptiness I am aware of is my stomach," Will said, rubbing his large stomach. "And a couple slices of pizza can fix that problem." He got up and jogged back on the court.

"Did he convert ya?" Colton joked.

"Shut up."

They continued playing ball. Christian watched them, knowing their constant criticism was just a defense mechanism to hide their vulnerability…their insecurities.

Colton shoved Will. "You getting sleepy, old man?"

They both laughed, and Will ran his big belly into Colton in return. "Nope. It's the emptiness." His mocking tone stung, but Christian refused to show it. Will stopped and put his hands on his knees, knowing the ball was coming back down the court.

Dominic hollered, "You need to lose that gut, man. Now c'mon, you're on my team." Will slapped his belly and winked at Dominic, then backpedaled as the shot bounced off the rim. AJ started running the ball towards them.

Mitch came out of nowhere and stole the ball. Will looked up, still panting, sick of running up and down. "What time is it?"

"It's almost four," Thomas said. All the guys slowed down.

"Oh, man. I can't miss my show, I gotta get home," Will said, as he walked over to the water bottles and shirts. He grabbed his bottle, drank and shot it towards the trashcan, leaving his arms up in midair. He missed and groaned as the guys laughed and ribbed him about his skills, and lack thereof.

Colton grabbed his shirt off the ground and put it on. "I have to jet too. I promised to be home by four." A few of the guys chuckled. It was not strange for Will to make an excuse about his shows when he was done playing. Colton always followed to go play his video games.

Colton and Will started walking out of the park together. They were quiet until they were sure the other guys were out of earshot. Colton spoke first, "Christian didn't even get mad. He's really changed."

Will nodded. "I think I liked him better before. Now he's all…dude, I can't even describe it. He's all happy Mr. Positive, Goody-Freakin'-Two-Shoes."

Colton shook his head, and laughed, "Something like that. Do you think it's real? He seems very sure of himself. I wonder if he's not a poser fakin' it."

"Do I think what is real?" Will looked over at Colton, who seemed lost in thought.

Colton met his gaze. "I don't know. Do you think he's fakin'? Do you think the stuff he says are real? That he doesn't feel empty sometimes, like ever? I mean, it's not like I need something, but he seems kind of chill n' happy all the time…"

Will shrugged. "I really don't know. I don't want to think about it anymore; Happiness is just sadness that hasn't happened yet… You wanna come watch something with me?"

"Maybe next time."

The two separated.

Will was going home to plop down in front of the TV, feeling connected to the shows he watched. Colton would be playing video games with online friends late into the night. The other guys had gone their separate ways, but Dominic stayed behind. He put both hands together and rubbed them. His eyes were tired, but vibrant with a nervous spark, glancing around to see if the coast was clear. Then he hurried over to where Christian was still sitting.

"Hey, can I talk to you for a sec...?"

"Yeah, what's up?"

"Uh… remember how you always talk about living a better life, man... Uh, are you sure that there is a better life for people like me?"

"What do you mean people like you?" Christian kept a defensive gaze on Dominic. He was used to being jabbed, so he remained ready to deflect a mocking comment but also give advice.

Dominic was clearly struggling to voice what was on his mind, so Christian attempted to make it easier for him, "If you want to talk to me, I can keep it to myself. I don't need to tell anyone."

Dominic looked up from kicking at the ground, "You swear? If anyone finds out, I'll know it was you, bruh."

Christian nodded, "You can trust me, I won't tell anyone."

"Oh, gosh, man," Dominic struggled to spit it out. Tears started to fill his eyes, "I've been keeping this to myself for ages but I need to tell someone before I blow up. It's a very old story and it's really embarrassing. I can't tell the other guys, but I kinda…I get the feeling you can really hear and understand. I've said these words in my head so many times and now I can't even get them out." He stopped to let out a breath, trying to get a grip of himself. "My…my uncle used to do stuff to me, man. It has caused me a million issues all these years. I can't even believe I'm talking to you about this, but I can't hold it to myself no more."

"I'm sorry to hear that, Dom. You know it's not your fault, right?"

"I haven't told anyone. I tried once, but no one listened …" Dominic's voice trailed off as he started to sob, dropping his head to hide the tears cascading down his face.

Christian looked away and started praying inside, *"God, show me how to help him. Give me the right words to say."*

Dominic took a breath, and it became clear why he chose this moment to talk about it. "You know my little brother -- what if he hurts my little brother like he hurt me? I can't let that happen, but I don't know what to do…"

Christian nodded, forcing his tone to stay calm. "You might need to talk to someone. Maybe an adult could help?"

"I tried."

Karen waited for Uncle Jim to show up that night to watch Dominic, while she went to school and then work, as normal.

"Jim, we need to talk," Karen said with a troubled look on her face.

Uncle Jim was unconcerned, even knowing what he had done two days ago. "Yeah, what's up?"

Karen asked him to sit down and handed him a cup of coffee. She didn't see little Dominic hiding behind the counter to listen. "Dominic told me something very disturbing. If what he told me is true, I don't care that you're my brother. I'll have you locked up."

Uncle Jim sipped his cup of coffee calmly, "What is it? You haven't told me what he said."

"He told me that you touched him."

Uncle Jim raised an eyebrow.

"Did you?"

"Karen - sis, you've known me our whole lives, and you know that isn't true! I'm dating Simone, why would I touch a little boy? You better get his imagination under control."

Dominic came out of his hiding place, and started screaming, "You know you did! You touched me like this!" Dominic showed his mom what happened, frantic for her to believe him. He couldn't believe his uncle would do something, then lie about it. "Tell her the truth! You did it!"

Karen's heart was sinking, but she was doing her best raising her only child by herself. Uncle Jim appeared unfazed by his outburst. He sipped more coffee then gently lay the cup aside.

"I ain't watching your kid if he's going to say stuff like this! I'm out, good luck!" Uncle Jim grabbed his stuff and started to leave. He knew she would never let him leave because she had no one else to watch Dominic while she was off at school and work. *"That's bull, and it's sick. Maybe somebody did something to him, but it wasn't me. Karen, you know better."*

"Wait, let me talk to him! I'll make sure he doesn't tell stories again. Jim please, I can't miss school or work!"

Karen grabbed Dominic's collar and hauled him into his room. He plopped down on his bed sobbing. Her heart ached; her instincts were yelling that something had happened to her little boy, but she couldn't figure it out and it was a lot to contemplate. One minute, life was normal, and the next her son was saying her brother was a monster. Part of her wanted to believe her son, but her brother was an adult and he was so calm and convincing. *"Baby, Uncle Jim is saying he didn't touch you. What happened?"*

"Momma, he did it like this." Dominic showed his mom again.

"Dominic, just stop that! STOP! I don't know what happened, but you must stop blaming your uncle! We'll talk about this later, but if I hear that out of your mouth again, you'll be in big trouble, do you understand me? You can get someone in a lot of trouble, making accusations...saying things that aren't true...that's what that means. Your uncle could end up in jail for a very long

time, and it would be all your fault. No more, do you understand me?"

"Mom, he did…"

Karen smacked Dominic across the face. She didn't mean to, it just happened. "Stop it! I have to go!" She instantly regretted the smack, especially when he was obviously going through something, but what was done was done. She hurried out to the kitchen where Jim was waiting. "I have to go to class, I'm sorry." She left.

Uncle Jim slithered into Dominic's room, promising to ruin Dominic. He was taking the abuse further, and something in Dominic withdrew. He died a little inside, and just knew that he couldn't trust adults. If his uncle was doing this, and if even his mom wouldn't listen to him, then maybe he was everything his uncle was saying. Worthless. A waste of time. A liar. Uncle Jim made it clear no one would believe him, so he decided to stop looking for help and just began to shut down as Uncle Jim slowly closed the bedroom door behind him.

"I shouldn't have said anything!" Dominic jumped to his feet and started to walk away.

Christian scrambled up and followed after him, "Dom, maybe you could talk to someone who could help. You're worried about your brother, so maybe someone else could talk to your mom and fix this."

"I'll think about it, but you didn't answer my question…is there a better life for someone like me?"

"Yes, of course. You aren't bad because something bad happened to you. Your uncle was wrong, not you."

"Man, you don't get it," Dominic stopped, and buried his head in his hands. "I've been trying to fill that emptiness you keep talking about. I been trying to collect more friends and working to put notches on my bedpost—with guys and girls, but nothing seems to work and sometimes I feel like I've ruined my entire life…"

"Guys and girls?" Christian thought to himself.

Christian's hand was on his shoulder, a gentle touch, not enough to spook him. He wanted Dom to know he was there for him without having to say it, "We all mess up. You can start over, ya know? You may not forget, but you need to stop allowing your mind to dwell on those painful memories; rest your mind in something better. You are precious and beautiful just as you are. Only love that can't be changed by our behavior has the power to change our behavior. Knowing that you are loved, accepted, precious and beautiful will help for the healing process in your heart and mind, then everything starts to blossom as you trust God and chat with Jesus every day."

Dominic frowned, "Please don't tell anyone what I told you. I get what you say, it just doesn't seem real. Not for me."

"You haven't tried it, Dom."

Christian had developed an endless patience for his friends. He wasn't always a very patient person, but he knew what was going on with them. He just wanted them to see the truth and he would keep on praying and pushing because he had seen what faith had done for his own transformation and they needed it too --- especially Dom. He didn't want Dom to walk away feeling hopeless.

"Look, I'm gonna be really honest. I might ask my pastor what to do in this situation, but without using your name because this is quite serious. Please think about speaking to him on your own. I know you love your little brother, man, and your uncle shouldn't be around him. Maybe Pastor could help by talking to your mom for you."

Dominic's face went from worried to plain angry, "Just stay out of it. I'm not kidding!"

Dominic headed off down the road, his heart racing. Christian felt his pain. Dom held this secret for years, and now that he has brought it into the light, he felt vulnerable. If another adult got involved, there could be trouble. They might have to tell the authorities, and then anything could happen. He was only eight years old the first time his uncle touched him. It started out like that and got way out of control. His mom didn't believe him when he told her. Maybe she didn't want to at the time. It would mean finding a new babysitter, making certain changes she was in no position to do. All those years, and he told nobody else until now. Dom wasn't asking for the world to be saved. He just wanted to be safe and keep his little brother away from his uncle's claws. It was a tough decision to talk about it. His emotions were running ever so wildly. Christian would have to watch his tone of voice and gesticulation so as not to give away the discomfort he felt with the secret he now carried. It was a heavy burden and he couldn't tell nobody else. If Dom's mom slapped him at eight for trying to tell, there was no telling what she would do now. One thing was for certain, neither Dom nor Christian would be getting any sleep that night.

CHAPTER THREE

It's Friday afternoon and the town of Vernon is replete with the usual hustle and bustle of inner-city life. Young men standing at a corner pressing weed into their palms, smoking, drinking, whistling at the scantily dressed females who stroll by enthralled by the desired attention. The air is pungent with the smell of stale cigarette smoke, uncollected garbage and the hotter than usual, stagnant summer heat.

JoJo's Pizza Joint sits at the corner of the community between two Hispanic pawn shops and draws a lot of community crowd. AJ and Isaac wave at Dominic through the smudge-free glass as he approaches the diner.

"Hey!" Dominic calls to AJ and Isaac as he slipped into the empty space at their usual booth. "What's new?"

"We were just talking." Isaac said, slurping on the last few drops of a large cup of root beer.

"About what?"

"What do you think about this empty space Christian has been rambling about all this time?" AJ asked.

Dominic rolled his eyes but not from annoyance. He was unsure whether Christian had kept his mouth shut. *Why would AJ ask this question out of nowhere?* He struggled to hide the defiance in his tone when he answered. "I dunno. What about you?"

AJ tilted his head from side to side, stretching, "I have no clue. But this morning's hangover got me thinking about a couple of things. Last weekend I was more high and drunk than I've been in a very long time and, I don't know, it struck me that maybe I wasn't having so much fun. What if the reason why I got so wasted was because I was trying to lose that void? I always think partying makes us all happier. I mean, it's fun - but then when I sober up, man, when I sober up, I find I got new problems and I'm becoming more aware of that empty place inside. These ups and downs are making me sick."

Dominic listened closely to see if AJ was talking about his secret, but it seemed as if he was talking about his own void.

The door chimed as Devin walked in. He walked over to their booth and flipped AJ's hat off before sliding into his usual space. Dominic narrowed his eyes at Devin as he picked AJ's hat up for him. "Piece of crap!"

Devin puffed up his chest with a sneer. "Who do you think you talking to, boy?"

The guys noticed a big scar on Devin's face.

"What's up with your face, bruh? You walked into a door again," AJ joked.

"Don't worry about it, bruh," Devin quickly dismissed him.

Christian walked in, all smiled. "Hey guys!"

Devin mumbled under his breath, "Great. Just what we need. Mr. Void himself."

Isaac waved back. "I'm glad you're here, Christian."

"Wouldn't miss it! Hey, guys."

"Hey, Christian. I was just telling Dominic that partying is getting old. I like getting drunk, it's fun. I like getting high, but man, I seem to need more and more to get that feeling. You always seem like you're having a blast. Where do you get it from?"

"Well, I am glad you ask. I like to go to youth group ---"

"Youth group… where is that and where is it located at?" AJ chimed in.

"Look, I'm only here because I was bored at home. I don't want to hear this crap. Doesn't anybody have a fun story to tell? Anyone got a hot chick on the go? I mean, didn't y'all go to a party or did something worth telling? We're young; I don't have time to act like old boring men."

"What's up with your face," Christian asked, noticing the scar.

"This don't concern you, man. Why you always acting so sentimental and stuff? It's utterly annoying." Devin said defensively.

AJ interjected, "I want to hear what Christian was gonna say."

"I don't, and if this is what y'all gonna be talking about, I'm gonna jack split." Devin said.

"Dude, chill! I want to hear it! We don't have anything going on for us. You're just as miserable as the rest of us," Isaac cut in.

Ever since Devin's dad went to prison, he has been acting street tough. Isaac was sick of it. Devin despised Isaac because he had both of his parents, and they were the richest family in the district. He was all set for life. His father was a doctor and his mom a professor. Isaac would go to college for free because his mother worked at the university. He had a bright future and Devin coveted that because he knew who his dad was, but he had never been in his life, so he didn't really *know* him. His mom worked her tail off to provide for her kids, and she was a classy lady, but things were still tough. The differences between Isaac and Devin were common knowledge and it kept them separated. Isaac knew he had things easier, but he still didn't approve of Devin's attitude towards the group. Having a difficult life didn't give him extra rights.

Devin had a special distaste for Isaac. He was from the hood, someone who had to struggle in life to get what he wanted, while Isaac inherited designer clothes, a big house and a nice car without lifting a finger.

Dominic wanted to fit in with Devin. He was still nervous about what Christian would do with the information he shared, "Can we talk about something else?"

"Shut up, Dom, you've still got the emptiness! Your relationships don't make you feel better and you know it. All the chicks you've left broken after promising to care for them… we all know that once they put their trust in you, as soon as you get what you want, you leave 'em. You need to hear this too!"

AJ was neutral in the Isaac-Devin fight, but he was not amused with Dom trying to act like Devin. The group can only take one member with that attitude. Dominic blushed, immediately defensive.

"Look, I know I've done some messed up things, alright. Sex worked for a while, I felt like a stud and all. I've ruined my chances of finding a girl to go out with properly. They've all been warned to stay away from me, so now no one wants anything serious. It sucks, but I can't change it now."

The other guys didn't know he struggled with homosexuality. He kept it a secret because they were always talking about gay guys being nasty. Their comments made him feel dirty about his sexual choices and he felt trapped by his bad decisions.

Devin sat all the way back, "To be honest…" he dragged it out until all eyes were on him, leaving them hanging, waiting for some epic pronouncement, "…the sex is definitely working for me." He started laughing very loudly.

Everyone rolled their eyes. The pizza showed up and they quit talking to pull slices from the pie. AJ took a bite, then shrugged. "I guess we keep looking. There's gotta be something out there to fix us. I'm not sure Christian has all the answers, but it seems interesting at this point. I might join ya at youth group soon, man."

Christian didn't hide the joy inside and answered with a huge smile, "I would love that. Just let me know when you're ready."

AJ glanced at his watch, "I have to go. See ya, guys." He dropped some money on the table and left.

Devin took out some of the cash and pocketed it.

"What're you doing, Devin?" Christian said, noticing Devin's swift movement.

"He left too much for tip, as usual." Devin smirked. The others just shook their heads knowing Devin's habit of just taking what he wanted.

Isaac was ready to ask questions. He had been reading up on religion. His family was not religious, preferring to look at life from a scientific standpoint, "Philosophy tells us a lot. Aristotle says that it takes a village to raise a child, and I think it's great you've joined a community that helps deal with emotions and feelings."

Devin started cracking up, "Religion…wow, y'all are wasting your time talking about this trash. I got 99 problems, but church ain't one. I'm going out for a cigarette. Y'all need to finish this convo while I'm out there."

Isaac sucked in a deep breath, so he didn't say something rude. Devin was bossy, always pretending like he was the leader of a gang. Isaac was disturbed by his attitude but he really wanted to have a conversation with Christian so he responded in a measured tone, "Devin, I'm not talking about religion. Do you even know what philosophy is? I reason that the emptiness isn't there, that it's a construct that gives Christians or whatever other group a way to convert people by convincing them they're missing something. I denied the void, but it became like denying a rock in your shoe."

"Bro, look, you just lost me. I need a smoke now," Devin stood up and headed outside.

Isaac glanced at Dominic and then Christian. "I've tried religion for the last three weeks but decided it makes it all worse. I felt the false hope that the emptiness would be filled if I could just keep the dang rules, if I could just do enough good deeds. My problem is that I have bad days and it feels like I lost all my progress. It's hopeless, and I don't know how you're happy all the time. You might be manic. Something is wrong with you, because your life sucks and yet here you are, smiling."

Dominic's eyes go wide, and his jaw dropped open, "Whoa, *what!?*"

Christian's life does suck but it was rude to point it out. His parents died in a horrific crash when he was too little to remember them. The sun was shining, and witnesses accounts say the young couple appeared to be arguing.

The car started to speed up until it veered off the road and into a tree. They were killed on impact. Christian was sent to live with his grandparents - and when he was eleven or twelve, his grandfather died. He was taking care of Christian and his wife with Alzheimer's. After he was gone, no one came forward to help. His grandma was put into a nursing home and Christian was bounced around from foster home to foster home until he ended up with a family nothing like him. Christian didn't ruffle at Isaac for reminding him, "Fair enough. You like philosophy, wait 'til you dig into the Proverbs and Ecclesiastes. I didn't understand certain things that happened in my life, but I trust the Lord has designed great plans for me."

Isaac couldn't understand what goes on inside Christian's head. None of his friends did. It almost appeared as if someone had brainwashed him and rewired his thought process. Even with the facts of his less than ideal life laid out on the table, all he had in return was a happy face. "And what if He doesn't? What if no one's up there? What if He's not listening? Does He even care?" Isaac swayed between amazement and annoyance that Christian could be so calm and shrug away the horrible things he had been through.

Dominic put his finger up to draw the attention of the other two and raised his chin towards the door. The other two were too deep in conversation to notice what was going on outside. There was a group of guys hanging around Devin. They were all wearing the same colors and they seemed a little shifty, looking around like they are watching for something. Devin looked inside and waved, then walked away with them.

Dominic shook his head, "Man, that's not good—those dudes are trouble. We need to go now."

They all knew the guys with Devin are older and members of the toughest gang around. Christian prayed silently as they left the diner.

§

Christian raced down the hall of the General Hospital. His mind was set on room 202. The door was open, and all his other friends were already present in the room. A few adults were standing outside the room, but Christian didn't stop long enough to see if any of them were familiar.

Devin was lying unconscious on the hospital bed, bloodied, unconscious and bandaged. Christian could hear the soft beeping of the machines he was hooked up to, but that was all he heard. His friend was lying in a hospital, fighting for his life and Christian knew he was not prepared for the world beyond. Mitch repeated her statement a few times before Christian's senses kicked in and he was able to hear the conversation.

"He's going to be alright."

"What happened?" Christian asked, almost in tears.

"He got in a fight and seems it was intentional."

"What do you mean, intentional?"

Mitch took Christian's arms, and pulled him outside the room. Once they were standing out of earshot from the others, Mitch sighed deeply.

"We think Devin is involved with some gangs. This was an initiation fight, and he lost."

"We have to do something."

"Devin is not taking advice from nobody. Mom talks to him, but he ain't listening to nobody."

"I don't understand what's going on with him."

"It's tough, bro, this life. I go off to college in September, and there's no money. Mom works very hard to make ends meet, and the ends still ain't justifying the means. Devin thinks he has a responsibility, and this is the way out. I believe his intentions are pure."

"This road goes nowhere, Mitch, except to prison or jail. Devin's our friend; he's your brother. We have to talk sense into him."

"If he survives the night."

CHAPTER FOUR

Christian lay awake in bed and all he can think about was his friends. He needed to find a way to reach them. As he glared at the pale white ceiling above his head, the faces of all his friends reflected back to him. They were as lost as Christian once was, but they couldn't even see it. Christian opened the group text with a message to meet at the court. "Bring your A-game. It's time to ball!" Basketball was the one thing they all still had in common, and it gave him a platform to talk --- or listen. It had been months since they hooked up, since Devin was finally released from the hospital with a concussion and a prescription for a high dosage of ibuprofen, and he had still not said a word to anyone about what happened. He had been going to the gym everyday and training really hard, but no one knew what he was training for.

Dominic replied almost immediately. "Can't make it today. Sorry."

Christian knew their last talk was heavy, so he just responded, "'k bro, next time." The teams would be uneven, so they would have to let him play.

Christian got there early. Will was already shooting around. They started playing shot for shot until Will said, "I've been noticing when I watch TV that I keep coming across these preacher men. I want to hear some real stuff from you. Can you tell me more about it?"

Christian went for a three-pointer and hit it, all net. Will high-fived him and they walked to get a drink, sitting on the bench by the court. "What do ya want to know?"

"How did you get rid of the emptiness? I mean, you used to be just like us, we all used to talk about it a lot. Remember? About how nothin' was making us happy. How life was useless. It used to be a joke for all of us, for you too. But now you seem as if there's peace inside you, like you're happy and fulfilled. How'd you do it?" Will looked into his bottle like it might have the answers.

Christian took a breath, "I don't deal with the emptiness anymore because I accepted the fact that Jesus is my Lord, my Savior and best friend. I have this relationship with Him that we all need, and this relationship is available for everyone. Father loves us all equally, and that's why I talk to you all about it. There is room for Him in every one of us and once you understand that His love is infinite, all that negative stuff just drops off. My adopted mom always told me that the entire creation is the object of God's affection, and He is not about to abandon what belongs to Him - the gift of His Son is for everyone to realize their origin in Him, who mirrors our authentic birth - begotten not of flesh, blood or water but of the heavenly Father. She is a sweetheart, a very passionate lady. Oh I love her dearly. She is convinced beyond the shadow of a doubt that God loves us to a degree to which we can't escape from it."

Will shook his head, "You be peddlin' some snake oil, bro. I'm trying to be real, and you're spinning some fairy tale, c'mon."

"I'm telling you the truth." Christian saw the other guys coming and he put his hand over his eyes to make out their demeanor. "We can talk about it later. Here they come."

Colton broke off from the others when he saw Will and threw his basketball into his chest, wanting their normal routine—for Will to pass him the ball under the net for his slam dunk. He and Will have been helping each other with some trick shots, and Will was bigger, so he practiced backward shots while Colton would go for the hoops. Will biffed the pass, and Colton spread his arms wide. "Dude, you left me hangin'! The hell... why you look like someone stepped on yo' dog?"

Will ignored him, so Colton tried Thomas, who was quiet all the time. Thomas threw the perfect pass. AJ couldn't help but toss his ball too, looking for a great pass. "Dude, set me up!"

Thomas liked to be involved, but he was unsure what to say to the guys. He was a watcher, and he had been listening to their conversations all summer with the same passive attitude he has had all his life. He sets AJ up and they started running through the court to warm up, practicing from the free throw line, doing half-court shots, just getting loose.

Isaac hanged back in the conversations too, and Thomas kept hoping they would become better friends. The other guys could be loud and ornery – it was fun and hilarious at times, but he wanted more serious talk. Thomas and Isaac were both quiet, but for different reasons. Thomas was naturally introverted. Isaac kept quiet because they already harassed him about his parents and his education. He was more concerned than ever about his place in the group, because he had applied to go to post-secondary this year, which meant he wouldn't be in classes with them. If he was accepted to the program, he would be heading to the local college campus for the rest of high school. His dad wanted to insist on this path, but his mother made it his choice. She swayed his opinion by pointing out that going this route would let him graduate college far sooner.

On the other side of the court, Devin was obviously in a dark mood. He wouldn't look his friends in the eyes and his gaze shifted constantly, as if he was suspicious. It changed the tone of the game, and none of them were as relaxed as normal. "3 on 3 dudes, square up." Mitch was a no-show, which was nothing strange. She liked hanging with the guys but prioritized doing chores and running errands for her always-busy mom. Devin was always missing in action and was unreliable and not very trusting with errands that involved money, so their mom preferred to allow Mitch to handle the family business.

Christian was again left on the bench but decided that he wanted to play a part this time and not just spectate. It was his idea after all. "I'll referee. So, everyone on the free throw line, knockout team pickin.'" Christian waited for someone to object, but none was forthcoming.

The guys went to the free throw line, throwing shots. As they missed, they went to opposite sides. Will went down, then Isaac, on and on until Devin and Colton were duking it out shot for shot. Devin missed and realized he was on the team with Isaac. "Dang. Preacher man reffing, and pretty rich boy on my team…let's get it over with."

Since they were the last men standing, Colton and Devin got to do the jump ball. They stepped up to the line and Christian threw the ball up between them. Colton went up and sent it to Thomas. Devin ran straight into Christian when he took off to defend his basket. Christian didn't say a word.

The banter begun with Colton. "Yeah, yeah, better than a video game."

Will jumped in. "Everything's better than a video game, except my movies. You do anything in real life, Colton? Or just pretend you bad in a game room?"

Colton backpedaled down the court because Isaac had stolen the ball. He was dribbling while Devin sets up under the net. Colton said, "Sure I do. I'm gonna play poker Friday. You wanna come? That's real. You gotta bring cash though."

Devin chimed in with, "I'm in. I got money."

Colton instantly regretted speaking. Devin could bring trouble to the poker group. He got nervous and sent a look to the other guys. "I can only bring one person. You coming, Will? I invited you first."

Will was focused on the ball, oblivious. "Nah, Devin can go."

The game continued for a few minutes without banter, passing the ball around without any real effort to move on the hoop. The air was thick, everyone feeling it, except Will. Eventually, Christian said, "Colton, didn't you say you were done gambling? I thought you lost it all before."

"I did but right after I won the gamer competition and had ten grand to play with." He shrugged, unconcerned. "Video games were boring me after all the practicing for the comp. I gambled a bit. It was fun, until I started losing. But I know what I'm doing now, so I won't lose it all. I'll be smart." Colton sounded confident.

"Did it make you feel better to gamble? Did it fix the boredom?"

"When I was winnin,' heck yeah! But once I lost - I got a bit depressed. I needed that money. But that's why I ain't going to the casino. I'm playing poker, and those dudes ain't gon' know what hit them. Once I'm up, I'm out."

"Hey freaks, are we playin' or what?" The game had slowed down, and Devin's mood was not improving. But Colton didn't like when people were mouthy with him.

"Bruh, you're free to participate in the conversation or not, but you can be respectful. We're just talking."

Christian wanted to keep Colton from joining a poker game, because Colton had the personality that took things too far. Christian knew Colton had been homeless. He had stayed with Christian's foster family before - not officially though, but he was bouncing around and staying with friends as long as he could, keeping below the radar by moving to the next guy's house for a few days at a time. Christian had figured it out and got him to stay longer. His mom was frequently in jail or high in a drug house. Everyone knew about his mom, but no one said much because he had a rough life. His dad raised him and did the best he could. He had been a jock in high school and wanted Colton to follow in his footsteps - but to go further and take it pro. Colton was more worried about collecting friends and being Mr. Popular.

"We can make plans for Friday, if you change your mind. We're going to go bowling. Anyone can come that wants to, and it's free."

AJ chimed in, "I haven't tried religion. I know it's about getting clean, some of the dudes talked about God and stuff. It didn't really help me, but it seems to be helping you."

Devin interrupted again with a strong pass. "Are you guys playing or just talking to God's holy referee over there?" But nobody payed attention to him because Christian was still talking.

"That's good it helped some of the people. It's not really religion though but an honest and true relationship. This relationship with God and me isn't based on rules and regulations that each of the party should fulfill in order to qualify, be loved or accepted in the relationship, but it is only based on pure love. I see it like this—life becomes complicated and difficult as we make choices. Sometimes, those choices aren't in alignment with the plans God has for our lives. We are all born innocent in our minds, but life gets off track as we try to do what we want."

Isaac caught on. "So, you're saying we feel this way because we are not living the life we are designed to live?"

Isaac was thinking about how he felt when his parents planned his future right in front of him. He went along with it, mostly because he didn't know how to say no to them. They paid the bills, and if he followed the path they set, they will fund his education. Who could say no to that? Maybe that was the path, and God - as Christian knows Him - set his parents to guide him. That doesn't explain the rest of the guys, though. If it did, they were at a real disadvantage, and that brought him back to his atheist views. *God couldn't exist because it doesn't make any sense, at all. He loves us so much that He lets some people have a chance to succeed, while others have the odds stacked against them.* It doesn't balance out in Isaac's mind.

Colton had been paying attention. "Dr. Christian and his Band-Aids for the crappy emptiness we all got. Christian has all the answers with his relationship…dude," he punched Isaac on the arm, "You buying this? Why don't we just play ball, man!"

Isaac rubbed his arm. "I want to hear what he has to say."

Christian was still smiling. "As far as I can tell, every human being experiences this illusion of having a void inside that can't be filled by anyone or anything, except someone actually becomes aware of the person, the finished work and the unending love of Jesus Christ. Our hearts are supposed to entwine with God's thoughts – and His thoughts should merge with our knowledge of Him, who saved us by grace through faith. Nothing else gets rid of that longing. No matter what you try, the outcome is temporary - like a Band-Aid. Most times the things we stuff in that 'emptiness' leave us worse off than before. We try to fix that feeling, that ache, and it takes a lot of work to chase things we can't control. Like gambling, you can lose it all, but it seems fun, until the games are over and reality sets in, and reality always sets in."

Devin bounced the ball, his tone hard. "I came to play ball, not hear you preach, dude. I'm really getting tired of this trend. Either we play…"

Isaac piped up. "Alright, alright let's play."

"Hey Christian, I see what you're saying. Tell us more." Colton looked right into Devin's eyes. He liked to push buttons, especially Devin's.

"Hey, hey, hey-" Will saw Devin's fuse was about to blow.

Isaac ignored it, focused on this conversation, "You know what, Christian, I tried that, to be honest."

"You did?" Christian said, raising his eyebrows.

"I did, and I'm telling you it didn't help me at all."

Christian nodded slowly, thinking it through. "Well, if you really did have a relationship with God, how come you still feel empty?"

"Because it didn't work for me. It's not for everyone, that's all." Isaac shrugged and his tone was decisive, like that was it. "I tried all the religions and none of them worked. None of them helped."

AJ whistled. "Whoa dude, you serious? *All* the religions?" He started cracking up.

Isaac turned to AJ, and everyone took a break as the conversation got heavy. "I did everything everyone told me to do, and I was left feeling like I wasn't doing enough."

Christian didn't want the others to misunderstand what was happening here. "Isaac, I'm not talking about a religion you use as a formula to fix whatever situation you may be going through. I'm talking about a personal and active relationship with Abba Father, Jesus and Holy Spirit."

Colton couldn't help himself anymore. "We are all sinners and God doesn't want to deal with us directly. We have to go through priests, prophets and pastors who are holy enough to represent us before God or order us to recite some 'Hail Mary full of grace,' because we are not worthy. You be sacrilegious dude, talking about this relationship with God bologna. Stop pretending we can all have a relationship with someone we aren't worthy to be near." Colton ramped all the way up and started trying to talk in a British accent, "Oh, please, I would like to go into the palace to see the Queen of flipping England. I am here to have a *personal* relationship with her, if ya know what I mean?" He snapped out of the voice and looked at Christian. "Seriously bruh, never happening. And it sounds stupid…that's what you sound like."

"That is absolutely incorrect! Who told you that?"

Colton ignored him and kept going. "And by the way, I don't have enough money to feed myself, but if I give enough money to the prophet or pastor, then I become eligible for the blessings of God. I don't qualify because I don't have money to buy some blessings from the preachers. That's cool, right?" The edge in his voice was getting sharper.

Christian knew this was imploding and raised his hands. "Guys, please listen to me. Money does not buy anything in God's kingdom. There is nothing humans can do to qualify themselves in the sight of Father, Son and Holy Spirit. The feeling of being empty can't survive when there's a clear understanding of who we really are in Jesus.

Colton couldn't stop asking questions. "Who am I?"

"That's a good question," Christian enjoyed the moment, "We are all sons and daughters of God. We were engineered by His design; He molded us in Jesus. We are His workmanship, His poetry, His permanent spiritual residence. We are part of His family."

"Oh okay, so, if we are part of God's family, why do we struggle with the void within us?"

"The only reason we go through whatever we go through in our soul or the reason we perish is simply because we don't know what God knows about us. Adam's mind changed, not God's. God never stopped being the lover of our souls. Even when we were lost, He found us and reminded us that we belong to Him before we were lost. What Jesus redeemed in everyone brings absolute closure and death to any other reasoning and judgment we may have of ourselves or anyone else. So, we are no longer supposed to know ourselves or anyone else according to our human or religious point of view."

The guys were hanging on Christian's every word.

"Hey Chris, this kind of sounds contrary to what a preacher who came to our house said one day." Colton continued.

Christian was trying to help his friend, "Oh yeah? what did he say?"

"He said that I couldn't benefit from anything the Bible says because I am not going to church. So, I felt like he was right."

"Meaningless conversation is often disguised in religious eloquence. Just because something sounds familiar or sincere, doesn't make it true. If my tongue is not bridled by what my heart knows to be true about myself, I am cheating myself and those influenced by what I am saying. God, who knew us individually, long before He formed us, is the same Engineer who knew every minute detail of our being as we grew mystically in the secret sanctuary of our mother's womb. He knows us now, and longs to introduce us to ourselves again, so that we may know, even as we have always been known!" Christian was trying to help his friends to see God the right way.

Isaac jumped in, "Everything you are saying sounds so simple, man."

Christian fired back, "That is what salvation is. Salvation isn't a reward for good behavior; it is an act of grace from start to finish, we had no hand in it. The gospel is the most dynamic and life-giving reality, cutting like a surgeon's scalpel, sharper than a soldier's sword, piercing to the deepest core of human conscience, to the dividing of soul and spirit; ending the dominance of the sense realm and its neutralizing effect upon the human spirit. In this way, man's spirit is freed to become the ruling influence again in the thoughts and intentions of the heart."

Christian stopped to take a breath, looking at each one of his friends in turn. "We are not the ones to make things right in our lives… *'not by might nor by power, but by my Spirit, says the Lord'*. We simply have to allow God to love us, and then we can respond to his love. He has the ability to lead us in exhibiting the quality of life we were designed to live."

Colton had seen televangelists asking for money in order to receive blessings from God, so he didn't understand how he could receive anything from God since he didn't have any income. "Man, everything you are saying is just amazing, but everything about me is just in bad shape. I wish I could be like Isaac, so I can get all the kinds of blessings I need to get."

Isaac felt bad when his friends spoke about his status, "Hey Colton, you know I don't really like to talk about the status of my family when we are together."

Christian jumped in before Isaac continued, "Guys, life's most relevant currency is contentment. We all should be grateful to God for who we are as individuals, friends and, above all, his sons and daughter. Also, to answer you, Colton, God's greatest resource on planet earth is vested in your innermost being. Instead of cluttering your mind with needs, budgets and bills, fill your thoughts with beautiful flowers and birds and consider how they live. God takes care of them and, remember, we are more precious to Him than they are."

Colton came again and asked, "Alright, I am sorry Isaac. Chris, is faith necessary? Because obviously the flowers and the birds don't have faith!

Christian answered, "Absolutely. But not as something you have to do in order to obtain something from God. We often think that faith is to believe things we do not understand. Blind faith is an illusion; faith sees what is! This is why Paul says that faith comes to you in the revelation of Christ. It is clear then that faith's source is found in the content of the message heard; the message is Christ. We are God's audience; Jesus is God's language; Jesus is what God believes about us. Faith comes out of the word that reveals Christ; the word of Christ. Herein lies the secret of the power of the gospel: there is no good news in it until the righteousness of God is revealed. God now persuades everyone to believe what he knows to be true about them. It is from faith to faith. The prophets wrote in advance about the fact that God believes that righteousness unveils the life that He always had in mind for us. Sin once called the shots, but now righteousness rules. God's faith defines life. The broody hen counts her chickens before they are hatched; she already sees them in the shell. If there is only one valid faith and one authentic source – No need to look any further - simply take sides with what God believes about you. He loves you, He has included you into His very life, He has blessed you with every blessings heaven can possibly enjoy." Isaac and Colton were amazed by the wisdom of their friend.

Devin was standing far back by the time he was done talking. "Hey, I'm out. I'm sick and tired of this crap. I show up to hang, not listen to a sermon. Christian, dude, hop off it. You ain't fixin' the world, and you will never change me. Knock it off or stay away from me." Devin took off. The others ignored him as he walked away.

Christian refused to let him go. He ran after him, and caught up to him, standing in his path.

"Hey, bro…" Christian had his hand in Devin's chest.

"Move, before I move you." Devin said, shoving Christian's hand off.

The other's had started to gather around, just in case intervention was required.

"You're my friend, Devin, and I love you man. That's all this is. I want our lives to count for something."

"I don't need your God for that. I can find my own way. Make my own path. Since my father died, I see my old lady working sixteen hour shifts just to make ends meet, and I ain't see no improvement. When dad was alive, we had everything. I want what he had."

"He was killed, Devin. That's the price he paid."

"He was stupid. I ain't gonna make the same mistakes he made. I'm gonna be better. The best."

"I saw you in that hospital room battering for life. We visited you every day, and you didn't even know we were there. Is that the life you want?"

"Move."

"No."

Devin punched Christian hard, and he toppled over in a heap, blood oozed from his nose. Colton and AJ grabbed Devin and stopped him from doing any more harm. Devin flashed them off.

"Y'all can stay here filling your minds with religious crap that will do nothing for yo'. I got better things to do with my time."

Devin walked off. Christian watched him go, wiping the blood from his nose as his friends helped him to his feet.

"That was a stupid move." AJ said.

"It was bold." Colton countered.

"Bold and stupid."

Christian silently watched Devin's form grow smaller down the street, knowing where the road he was on was going to take him.

CHAPTER FIVE

Colton had his own game room at his house where the guys usually gathered to play video games, lounge, or watch newly released movies. His father was passed out in the adjoining room from a hangover. His mom was probably at some drug house getting jacked up. Whether the parents were home or not made no difference to Colton when he and his friends were in his virtual world.

Isaac was busy replenishing their stack of snacks and drinks, before sitting down beside Will and popping a big bag of Doritos.

Colton and AJ were role playing a scene from the World of Warcraft video game. Colton was an expert at the game and needed very little concentration to move around and interact with his surroundings. AJ had to utilize all his mental faculties to try and keep up.

Colton asked, without taking his eyes off the screen, "So, based on what you have been saying, Chris, it doesn't matter if we are the most horrible people on Earth?"

Christian was responding to text messages on his phone, while watching the action on the television screen. "Those you call 'horrible people' were in God's mind when He was saving His creation from auto destruction. Jesus said, 'I am the way, the truth and the life, no one comes to the Father but by me.' He wasn't being exclusive; this is the most all-inclusive statement embracing all humanity. Here is what He was saying, 'I am [*you are mirrored in me*] your way; I am your truth and also your life. Every single person is now brought face to face with my Father entirely because of my doing.'"

Isaac wanted Christian to understand that he approached this closeness to God thing intellectually and put in effort. "I tried Christian. I really did - and it didn't work. I tried good works. Followed the rules, observed rituals. All of it. It was painful to not see results, like reading and reading and writing a great report, only for the teacher to call it garbage."

What it really felt like was his parents telling him to choose between a law degree and being a doctor, if he wanted them to pay for his education. In their estimation, anything less than one of those professions was a waste of their highly educated money. Isaac wanted to enjoy life, explore, travel, and create the paintings and art in his head, but they wouldn't hear of it. They were never proud, and when he displayed perfection with a straight A+ result, they acted like he just did what he should. There were kids whose parents got excited over C's. He longed to see pride in their eyes, instead of expectation or disappointment. He longed to see them more, outside of the brief family meetings that felt more like a business meeting for the family corporation. He wanted them to get excited for who he was, not what he accomplished. He had searched for this God Christian seemed to know, and he had spent what he considered to be a lot of time trying to earn God's love. He had sat for hours at night trying to feel different, full inside, happy, and he would find out that the more he travelled down this path, the more he felt emptier. He gave up just a few weeks later.

Christian can see that Isaac was experiencing an avalanche of emotions, so he boldly said, "You tried those things because we tend to understand God based on personal experiences. I have had this illusion of being empty myself, so I know the problem is simply ignorance."

"I feel like if I didn't do everything right, He would throw me into the fire without even hearing me out." Isaac couldn't hide it anymore. This had been eating at him for a long time. Isaac could feel the cracks inside, synonymous with the crackling sound of the Doritos he bit down on.

"Dude, legit, my grandpa used to tell us we were gonna burn in hell for everything we do wrong. He said it most when we didn't pray before eating." Will couldn't help being interested in this part of the conversation. Hell showed up in a lot of shows and movies lately.

The guys were all munching on snacks, playing the game of warcraft or just enjoying the spectacle of what was happening on the screen, while listening or participating in the back and forth. Devin was absent, so the defenses had come down a little.

Christian relished the opportunity to speak to his friends. For the first time he was saying the deeper things he couldn't just spout before. "That's the problem. The world didn't reject the real Jesus, it's the Jesus the present church portrays that the world is rejecting. The real Jesus is loving, and He accepts people just as they are. God is love, and everything that comes from Him is an expression of His love."

Isaac was nodding without even realizing it, his expression thoughtful.

"His love is unconditional because it is not based on how good or bad we are, but on how good Jesus has been on our behalf, once and for all." Christian could see Isaac's eyes opening.

"That sounds good man, but ya know, nice fairytale. I have to go." AJ was supposed to be helping with yard work today, so he had to get home. He handed the control over to Will. He was tired of playing the game anyway.

AJ thought he already lived in hell. His dad was an alcoholic, and if his dad was happy, there were no bruises to explain. If his dad was angry, life became unbearable, a true hell on Earth. His mom was usually there too, but she was always too high on prescription pills to stop his dad. AJ wasn't sure what to do. He could whup his dad, but even the thought of it made him feel guilty. Christian made that point about God being Father. He started thinking to himself, *"If God is that loving as a Father, maybe I need Him in my life."* But it was hard admitting that he wanted to drop the façade and say he wanted what Christian had.

"Bye, AJ." Will was usually the first to bow out. "He has a point there though."

Colton started laughing. He was in a fighting mood after the episode with Devin. "I thought you guys win people for God by making them make decisions out of fear to join churches."

"C'mon, Colton, choices made out of fear are not beneficial to anyone. My Grandma taught me about making the right decisions in life. She used her own experiences to show me how 'fear decisions' and 'growth decisions' affected her entire life."

§

Grandma was a business lady in her late twenties. She had always had some success in her company but a time came when she had so much competition in what she was doing, she was afraid to lose her biggest client, and see her company fall apart. So, she let the owner of that company yell at her repeatedly until she realized that there were only two types of decisions: those made out of fear and decisions made out of growth.

Only those two options remained in her mind. Should she have stayed in a job because she was afraid she wouldn't get another job? Or should she have stayed because she was excited about the potential for growth there? Should she have stayed in a relationship because she was afraid she wouldn't meet someone else, or she was afraid it would be bad for the kids, or was she afraid of hurting someone else? Or should she have stayed in a relationship because she was truly grateful the other person was in her life?

She thought about it. She picked all the major decisions in her life and shared them with Christian. She had moved to NYC for a job with the Company of Premium Cable and Satellite Television Network of Home Box Office, Inc. She left the Company of Premium Cable and Satellite Television Network to start her own company. She got married the first time. Then divorced. She got married the second time and got divorced again. She had kids from both marriages. She moved 80 miles out of NYC after losing her home and money. She tried to sell her company before it had fully bloomed. She always refused to take business trips because she was nervous about what would happen if she left home.

Every decision she made had either been fear or growth; not just big decisions but even the smallest decisions. The fear-based decisions never worked out for her. When she made a fear-based decision, it was always because she was giving power to someone else. She would make a fear-based decision out of insecurity; out of a feeling of scarcity; out of giving too much power to others, and they shaped her experiences in life because of that. The growth-based decisions all resulted in miracles she could not have imagined.

Growth-based decisions are felt in the body because there is an expansion of perception, ideas, feelings of competence, freedom and confidence. A growth-based decision becomes a story that needed to be told. A fear-based decision turned into regret.

Grandma listened to one of her first bosses yell at her so many times because she was afraid he would fire her if she argued. She didn't want to get fired because she had a company on the side and Premium Cable and Satellite Television Network was the biggest client. She had no confidence in her company. The fear of losing a client prevented her from devoting all her time to the real growth in her life.

She was afraid she was going to go broke again, so she took a job. She tried to convince herself it was a growth decision. Maybe she would expand at the job and create opportunities. The first day at the job she fell straight to the ground for no reason. Everyone laughed and asked, "Are you OK?" She got up because she was ashamed and embarrassed at all the people looking at her. She started to limp because she hurt her leg so badly.

The second day at the job, the boss of the company told her, "Trust me on your salary. We'll take care of you." She was afraid to argue. He was the boss. The third day at the job, she got up and walked out. She didn't clean out her office. She left her jacket there. She took the elevator down 40 stories. She walked out into the sun and she never went back. They called repeatedly. Even years later the main guy was still calling. Her life was better than ever. She never looked back. She left the building and walked to Grand Central. She took the train 80 miles. She watched the leaves turning from green to red along the way across the Hudson River. She came to her house and walked the one block to the river and breathed in the air not knowing how, what, why, and not thinking about money for the first time in months. Then she noticed she wasn't limping. Her leg didn't hurt. Not everything went good for her after that decision. Some pretty awful things happened. Her heart tore open more than once. Her fears about money came back again and again but it was a growth decision. Bit by bit, the growth decisions added up. She grew to love her life more than she ever had.

The boys were all quiet, attentive as they listened to what Christian learned from his grandma before he was taken to the family that adopted him. Will and Colton didn't notice that their characters on the screen was being mutilated by the enemy. Their focus was on Christian.

Will nodded. "Great illustration, man."

Christian nodded too, "Perfect love expels fear without leaving any trace of it. Fear holds on to an expectation of crisis and judgment, which brings separation, and interpret it as due punishment. It echoes torment and only registers in someone who does not realize the completeness of their love union with God. Being afraid is actually an indicator of the absence of the awareness of God's love and affection for you."

Isaac shaked his head, "If my relationship with God wasn't built on rules and rituals or good deeds, what do we need to do to experience His presence with us, and be all happy-go-lucky every day, like you?"

"I'm out. I'm gonna go relax and watch something easy. Peace." Will turned to the screen to notice that the game was over. He handed the remote to Isaac as he got up to leave.

Christian could see they needed to finish up before it overwhelmed everyone, and they pushed it away. "Look, when we put our hand in Jesus' hand, He holds on and won't let go. He ALONE can and WILL fill the emptiness y'all talk about. The patterns of our desires are shaped like Him. I am convinced that we are designed to enjoy the benefits of being born again by aligning our thoughts and minds with what God believes about us. Whenever we don't, we end up like Adam who, as soon as he did what he wasn't supposed to do, he put on another identity. He started to see himself from the wrong perspective. What happen most of the times is that we assume the wrong identity by saying things about ourselves that God doesn't say… like 'I am not good enough, I am not lovable, I am not smart, I don't look good, I am poor, I am possessed, I am not beautiful, etc.' The truth is that you are good enough, loved, smart, beautiful, etc. It is crucial to understand that we belong to God. We speak the contrary of what God thinks when we are trapped in the darkness [any opinions that suggest anything that isn't what God says about a person] and in our darkness and pain, we conclude and accept that I AM NOT and become addicted to that mindset. That's all!"

All the guys took the cue. Lost in thought, they started to mentally drift in different directions as Will sashayed towards the front door.

Dominic inserted his key into the front door lock of his home, still uncertain of what to expect when he went inside, trepidation rising in the pit of his stomach. Even though it was summer, mom still insisted on having his uncle come over to babysit his baby brother, Marc, on the evenings she had classes. He still struggled to be in the same space as his uncle because of what he did to him when he was younger, and he felt helpless to protect his little brother when his own mother thinks he was making the whole ordeal up. It was very painful for him to come home at the end of the day and little Marc had been acting strangely, signs and symptoms that he knew very well from his past experiences. History was repeating itself, and Dom felt powerless to stop it.

Dom walked into the living room, his back turned to the room as he closed the door, leaning against it. He knew that once he turned his face around, he had to face whatever it was that was waiting for him. In the quiet of the semi dark room, he heard soft sobbing. Instinctively he reached for the light switch and flipped it. Karen was curled up on the sofa, sobbing quietly.

"Mom!"

She didn't respond, but he knew something was amiss. He walked over to her and took her head in his hands.

"Mom, talk to me."

Karen sat up and tried to compose herself. It all happened so very quickly, but it was nothing unfamiliar. She had been there before but choose to omit what was obvious because she felt she had no choice.

"Marc just told me the same thing you told me when you were eight."

Karen was unable to control her grief. She knew her choice may have impacted her boys more than she was willing to admit, and she was indebted to them for any scar her turning a blind eye may have inflicted on their young lives.

"I didn't listen when you told me. I didn't want to hear. I was too focused on me, and still am. Dom, what have I done?"

Dominic embraced her. There were no words he could find in this moment, and his only thought was to kill his uncle.

CHAPTER SIX

Christian had been having a re-occurring dream at nights. One of his friends died…shot. People die in his community all the time because of gang-related clashes, but he never saw his friend's face. He had no idea who the victim was. He always woke up just before a face or further details was revealed. He didn't know if he should interpret the dream literally or it was symbolic for some other occurrence. But he cannot ignore the urgency he sensed inside after waking up. He looked at the clock by the side of his bed. It was almost midday. He was up almost all-night interceding for his friends. He doubted he was doing enough to get through to them and hoped God had His own plans to reach them. He checked his phone. It was Friday. He was hoping someone had taken him up on his offer to attend the Youth Group outing. No messages.

Christian got out of bed and made his way to the kitchen. His foster mom, Susan, was busy making pancakes and scrambled eggs.

"Good morning, sunshine," Susan said in her usual, charming and pleasant demeanor, "Did you sleep okay?"

"Another nightmare."

"You've been having a lot of those."

"Yeah. I'm really concerned for my friends."

"Knowing you, I bet you are doing your best to help them."

"I don't know if I am reaching them."

"Your responsibility is to plant the seeds in love. Don't worry about the harvest." Susan handed Christian a cup of orange juice.

"Where's Jim?"

"They are starting a new contract on the other side of town. He's trying to get in some extra early hours to seek favour from the head contractor, and hopefully get some extra hours in. We need the overtime."

"I don't know why he doesn't start his own construction company."

"We can't afford to risk starting a new company now and it doesn't work out with you so close to going to college."

"I really appreciate you guys."

"Do you remember when we first met?" Susan asked, lovingly as she placed a plate of pancakes and eggs on the counter in front of Christian.

"I try not to."

"You were lost, searching, confused. You saw life as an enemy, void of meaning and purpose."

"I lost everything I loved, without explanation."

"But look at you now. You lost everything, but you gained everything back."

"You showed me the way."

"I could never for the life of me fathom how you had a name like 'Christian' when you were a partaker of the mistaken nature, but you have proven to us and the world that we are not defined by our past; that there is hope in Christ for anyone to live His life. You taught us that! Today, you are a beautiful epistle; a love letter of Christ to the world, perfectly readable and plainly understandable by all; you are a superb adornment of God's love. Never stop touching people around you with your life. Extend God's welcome to them and provoke them to come and join in the celebration of what grace communicates in the person, love and life of Jesus Christ!"

"That is very sweet of you, ma'am. You are a great inspiration to me; I love you dearly."

"I love you more, my love."

"You know what… I ask Holy Spirit every day to speak to my friends through me. I fear each one of them is caught in the grip of the darkness within, they are going through the valley of death and I can't stop them."

"Righteousness, Christ in your friends is not measured by how you think or what you see now… remember, they all belong to Papa and He always finds His way to remind us of our origin. Your words are not futile. Love on them more and more and leave the rest to the One who loves them to pieces!"

"Amen, ma'am. You always have the right words for me when discouragement tries to rise."

"You are adorable. Come on, finish eating."

§

Devin was on his way to Colton's around lunchtime. He was trying not to miss the poker game. He stopped at a vendor and purchased two cigarettes. He checked his wallet to see how much money he had. *One hundred dollars. That should be enough.*

"Man, whatcha doing here so early?" Colton asked glaring at Devin standing on his porch.

"You would leave without me if I wasn't here on time," Devin said pulling on the last of his cigarette and flipping the butt onto the neighbors manicured lawn. The houses were too closely knit together to know where one boundary stops and the other begins.

"You shouldn't do that," Colton said as Devin invited himself in, and walked past Colton into the house.

A few blocks away, a few of the other guys were starting their day. Isaac had spent a couple of days mulling over everything Christian had explained. Then he invited Christian over for the day. Isaac was still doubtful and thinking about what the correct thing to do was because

Christian's ideas were not completely fulfilling, and he was proud of his analytic mind. Ever since he was little, he had always believed only in the things that fully convinced him. He was used to doing research and diving into topics. Filling his own void was no different, so he wanted to fully engage and interrogate the person who knew most about it.

Christian had made sure that AJ could join them since he finally decided to go to the youth group outing that night as well. Christian was happy that two of his friends were joining him. He had prayed all week that they would like bowling with other Jesus freaks and see that loving God wasn't boring or lame.

As soon as Christian rang the doorbell, Isaac opened the door. "Hey, come on in."

AJ and Christian walked in and looked around. It was always an experience to come to Isaac's home. His parents were wealthy, and his mom liked to redecorate the foyer to reflect a museum quality. She had new sculptures of humans that looked hand carved. There were tribal masks on the wall and amazing prints on pillows sitting on the regal chairs she always had available for guests to sit on while taking off their shoes. The zebra hide on the floor looked authentic. "That real, man?" AJ asked pointing at the floor.

Isaac huffed. "It's all real. Straight from Africa. She went over to get some research info from a colleague and came back with all of this stuff."

"Amazing." Christian loved the way Isaac's mom did things. It always made him long for his birth mother. Susan did her best to not make him feel neglected and unloved, but no one could truly replace the woman who bore you in her womb for nine months. Christian always liked seeing what other moms were like. Isaac's mother was a beautiful lady, calm and well educated.

"It's cool, dude," AJ added.

Isaac´s hands were shaky because he had been waiting for this moment and piling up questions. The last thing he wanted to talk about was his mom´s interior design skills. "I didn't invite you over to talk about my mom's stuff."

Christian looked Isaac in the eye and realized he had been waiting all day for him to get there. "What do you want to talk about?"

"Why does God tempt us and when we fall in sin, make the emptiness creep back in?"

The smile didn't move from Christian's face. He answered in a kind tone. "God cannot be both the source of light and darkness. God's gifts are good without exception, their perfection cannot be improved upon. You can't just keep doing things you know are wrong, thinking you are living the life that God designed for you."

Isaac's curiosity was sparked. The more he heard about Jesus, the more questions he had. Isaac listened carefully but it still didn't click into place, so he went at it again. "I don´t know the difference between the God-designed life and mine. I don't see where the void I feel comes from."

"A person's selfish desires are set against the Spirit, and the Spirit is set against one's selfish desires. They are opposed to each other. Any thought or action that isn't inspired by love will always hurt, divide, harm, destroy or kill. The heart is deceitful when we are not led by love so we must allow love to lead or inspire everything we do or say, regardless of whether we receive love back or not."

Isaac raised an eyebrow. It was a lot to take in and it was obvious that Christian knew more than he was saying.

Christian continued, "God doesn't make people shoot up heroin. He doesn't trick someone into drinking every night. Those are selfish desires that lead us to self-corruption." He took deep breaths between sentences, spoke slowly and freely. He doesn't want to upset AJ, but he couldn't think of other examples to show what he meant. These were the only ones that came to his mind and he could see they haven't reached him, because he was more and more nervous, breathing too fast but then he chuckled, and said tightly, "Don't lie, Christian, clearly God made my dad the jerk he is…he's too fresh like that to not have been made that way."

AJ was going through a tough time with his family. He loved his dad, but he hated him too. He was a cruel man, who often said terrible things about AJ and his mother. AJ believes his mom was the pill-popping mess she was because his dad was abusive in every way possible. He had only been physical a handful of times, back when his mom was halfway normal. Once she started being in a drug-induced fug every night, he reverted to telling her what a loser she was. He picked on his son and always found a way of treating him like a burden, a weight around his neck that stopped him from living. AJ was hurt by his dad's comments, and though he didn't want anyone to notice, they were slowly cutting a deep hole in his self-esteem. His father often said out loud that his family was the biggest mistake he had ever made, and that he was wasting his life—he could be having so much fun, if he didn't have to pay bills. AJ hardened his heart so he didn't cry but couldn't confront him about it. He just walked away or lowered his head. His mother took another pill. It was not illegal. She had prescriptions for everything she took.

Christian shaked his head. "I promise your dad did that to himself. You don't have to be like him."

AJ felt the tears rushing to his eyes, so he looked around, walking to each painting on the wall and inspecting them while he listened.

Isaac was still skeptical. In his view, there were not enough foundations to make the drastic affirmation Christian had. He wanted to know how to draw God's attention to him; he was seeing a selfish vision of Salvation but was not completely convinced it was feasible. He looked into Christian's eyes, as if everything around them did not exist.

"Basically, you're telling us there is nothing we can do to shock God. Does that mean we can't impress Him or convince Him to fill the void in us?"

Christian responded calmly again, but with a big smile. He knew where Isaac was coming from, because he was in his shoes once too. "There is no way to be impressive enough or convincing enough."

Isaac's jaw tightened, and his eyes narrowed. He felt Christian was hiding the answer on purpose. How was it right that there was nothing he could do to earn the freedom Christian had? He knew that deep inside, he wanted that peace of mind - and his friend was saying it was impossible.

Christian struggled to find better words and not lose the attention of his friends or annoy them. He started speaking calmly again. "When you hear something's free, it means you don't need to give anything to get it. It's a gift. Jesus stood where we couldn't stand as the man, representing all men, in receiving the gift that He is. There's no part for you to play. The ceremonies are over. We are invited to the party of the Godhead as new creatures, because of Jesus Christ. The work is over, finished. Any human being can receive this gift by faith."

AJ knew the answer but asked anyway so he could bring up a topic that was bothering him. "Even Devin, man? He's getting bad and I notice that we are trying hard not to bring it up. We all know what he's up to."

Christian turned and nodded. "Even Devin. Especially him. All fell short because of Adam, the same 'all' are equally declared found because of Jesus Christ and even before we were born. We were not made sinners by our own disobedience; neither were we made righteous by our own obedience. The same humanity represented in the one man, Adam, is triumphantly represented in the one man, Jesus Christ. Adam's transgression no longer holds the human race hostage!"

AJ didn't understand, but he smiled anyway. It was nice for him to be told he was special. His dad had been saying he would never be anybody and that he was a weight around his neck. Hearing something different sounded very good to him. Christian spoke in a firm, measured tone and he definitely seemed convincing to AJ. He wasn't joking.

Isaac's curiosity was lit all over again. He was not used to only half understanding what he was told, so he asked, "How was I found in God before I was born?" Even when he knew every single word in the sentence, he didn't get the meaning and Isaac always wanted to understand.

Christian flipped through the Bible and found a specific verse. He read, *"I knew you before I formed you in the womb; I set you apart for me before you were born; I appointed you to be a prophet to the nations."* Christian remained focused on his Bible as he found something else to read. He had been trying to retain his many Scripture references. He struggled in some subjects, but he was learning the Bible and it made him feel good to share it with his friends, "*...before the foundation of the world He chose us to become, in Christ, His holy and blameless children living within His constant care.*"

"I'm not good enough," Isaac rebutted. He could feel a pulling inside him. He wanted to understand it all, and his mind was going in directions he would have never imagined. He had struggled with his parent's plans for him, and yet he didn't really know himself. He thought he wanted to focus on the arts, but there was something new stirring in his heart, ideas he had never considered, dreams he dared not voice at this point. His face went still as he tried to make sense of these newly discovered lands in his own brain.

Christian smiled. "It *is* weighty. It changed my life."

AJ had heard every word. "Do you really think God gives freely?" His mind was trying to process the idea of a non-economical reasoning. The laws of the market and present economy did not apply to Jesus' giving and caring. It was difficult to understand because "free" was a rare concept these days in any culture.

"The love of God is unconditional. It is not our response to Him that attracts His attention. We have always had His undivided affection."

Christian finished his speech and looked at his friends, hoping for acceptance in their eyes. He knew deep inside he was telling the truth, telling them exactly how Jesus lit his path every day. "The sense of emptiness in the heart or soul indicates that someone is living a mistaken life, from a mistaken identity or going against the true self or heading in the wrong direction. There is more that we can ever want, think or imagine in the life God designed for us. Jesus is our all and there's no space inside us that He can't fill. He is ALL; EVERYTHING in ALL."

AJ exhaled slowly, gathering his thoughts. "If God loved me, my parents wouldn't be like they are. If His plan is for how things are at my house, then that's JUST messed up."

There was no understanding or acceptance in AJ's face, and his smile turned mocking. Christian understood that pain. He didn't have his parents, but it was not God's fault. It was easy to blame God at times, to turn the finger pointing at the Almighty, because He does have the power to stop or start things whichever way He wanted. Christian took a breath, still calm and collected. He had been in the same place AJ was now, so he understood the resistance. "God won't force you to participate in the one and only life He made available for you. But if you give up trying to make your own way, the feeling of being empty will be turned into a radiant joy of total satisfaction in every area of your life. It's that simple."

"You sound crazy." AJ's annoyance was clear. He wanted to believe it was that easy, but in his experience, nothing was.

"I feel like my life matters now is all I'm saying and what I have can also be yours."

Christian knew he had hit nerves in both of his friends and was very happy about it. He felt that the more he spoke to them about his own awakening, the more he understood it. He saw the changes he had undergone in the past few months, and it amazed him. The confidence he spoke with about these matters made him feel good, and he believed they would soon participate together with him in the faith of Jesus Christ, before it was too late.

"I'm getting hungry, is anyone else hungry?" AJ changed the subject because he felt like breaking down. He felt sorry for himself, but he had forgotten that Christian didn't have his parents at all. His foster parents did their best, but there was really no substitute for one's real parents. Although his family life was not good, it could be worse. He was sick of accepting the status quo, though. He wanted life to change, and fast.

Isaac focused and jumped into action, leading them into the kitchen. "My mom had sandwiches made, and fresh fruit, and veggies and dip. Sorry it isn't more exciting, she's a health nut."

The sandwiches were cut into dainty triangles, the condiments spread evenly on the side, each crust cut off. The fruit was cut into perfect bite size pieces, and the vegetables arranged into a design. The whole table looked like a picture taken from a design magazine.

All the guys secretly wished they had Isaac's fancy life, his car, his house. He only walked in summer because he enjoyed the exercise. He had opportunities the rest of them would never encounter but they knew better than to talk about it. He was still nice though, and always had been. Despite all the high-class things that surrounded him, he was the same boy he had always been; a caring friend who would be happy to help any of them. Isaac had a good heart and just as Christian might wish for his easy life, Isaac wished he had Christian's spiritual life. When he admitted it to himself, Isaac knew that happiness was not found in material possessions, but in transcendental love.

§

Devin and Colton didn't speak as they walked. The day had proved the gulf between them was widening. Colton played his video games, as he had planned to all day, until the poker game, and Devin brooded because he didn't really want to hang out with boring old Colton. He enjoyed his new crew far more than his old friends. They might have been friends since they were in elementary school, but Devin felt himself outgrowing them. They could stand around and talk about the dumbest stuff for hours. He had enough of it. He was ready for something with older and more interesting people.

Devin really hated Christian. *Why were people even giving him the time of day? Everything Christian ever told them was an absolute lie. Okay, there was a change in him, but he had to be faking. He was a poser and wanted to attract everyone to the church because he had been asked to.* Devin's anger blinded him from seeing the real change in his other friends too.

His new crew played hard. He was still living the high from the last party they had. If he closed his eyes and thought back, he could hear the music thumping, and see the way the chicks were playing up to the guys and not the other way around. It seemed perfect; it was where he belonged. Whenever he showed up, there would be alcohol and weed, people chilling and dancing. He could make money with them, fund a good lifestyle. When they trust him enough, they would let him in on their jobs and he would be set for life.

Devin knew he could be a leader with this crew someday. He was proud to wear the clothes he was given. The colors show other people what he was about, and even the adults that used to run their mouths at him were backing off. Belonging to a group gave him strength he could feel just walking the streets. He was no longer one guy on his own, he was a part of something bigger and it felt awesome. The only regret he had was not joining the gang sooner. He wasn't official yet, just a recruit, but he was determined to earn his stripes. He always said he would never be like his dad, but he got it now. He thought he understood why his dad did the things he did. He must have felt awesome when he joined a gang too. This was the path. His dad was a well-known thug, who was murdered while he was in prison for murder, and Devin had so much street cred on that alone. It might have been a source of shame with his old friends, but it was a medal of honor on his chest with his new crew. The gang knew his dad - and if Devin was honest, he was scared they would expect him to live up to his old man's behavior. He knew he could never hurt anyone like that but there was plenty of other stuff he could do.

"We're here."

Devin didn't know poker like Colton, so as they walked in, he imagined sweeping everyone at the table. He looked around once they were inside, making sure he was aware of his new surroundings.

§

Isaac Senior and his wife were enjoying a moment on the couch watching television, which is a rare occurrence. Both have just completed a major milestone at their companies, and have taken a day off for themselves, which they hoped to spend at home with Isaac discussing matters of his future. Both had a rough life growing up, but they believed in human potential enough to go after their dreams, when everyone around them was more concerned with the latest trends and the pleasures and passions of human emotions and desires. They studied hard when their peers were partying, smoking and living it up. They were very familiar with the power of socialization and peer pressure and tried to push their son beyond his own pre-conceived limits, being fully aware that it could be interpreted otherwise.

"Maybe we should just let him know that we are waiting to talk to him," Irene suggested.

"But we don't know how he's gonna take the news. You know how these young people are with summers and spending it with their peers."

"This will be good for him, and beneficial to his future. We have to make choices based on future benefits. Isaac needs to be better than we are."

"That's a lot to put on a kid."

The pitter patter of footsteps were heard and Isaac Junior appeared at the bottom of the stairs, dressed and ready to go.

"Oh, we had no idea you were going out," Irene said, glancing at Senior, "We were looking forward to talking to you about something."

"Can we talk when I get back?"

"How long you gonna be, son?" Senior asked, removing his glasses to get a good look at his son.

"Maybe two hours. I'm going bowling with Christian. His church has this outing thing going on."

"Church?" Irene asked, her eyebrows raised and knitted.

"Yea, so I will talk to you guys as soon as I get back." Isaac said and raced out the door.

Irene and Senior glanced at each other, unsure of what to make of their son's demeanor.

Senior finally said, "Cancel his next doctors' appointment. We are taking him to a psychiatrist."

$$\S$$

Alberto Bowling Alley was bustling with activities from the parking lot, extending all the way inside as church folks filed in trying to get a park, and joining the line to go inside. Christian, AJ and Isaac were among them moving closer towards the entrance.

"All these people your church peeps, man?" AJ asked, looking around at the multi-ethnicity, multi-nationalities, old, young and indifferent standing around.

"Yea,"

The doors were wide open, inviting everyone in. Young adults and old were pouring through the doors, while inside people were laughing and talking. The whole place had a relaxed vibe, with an atmosphere of fun and caring. They could all feel it. AJ and Isaac had been to a Bowling Alley before, but it felt a lot less "churchy." AJ found himself losing the mistrustful thoughts from earlier, replaced by happiness. Isaac felt the energy as well. He was surprised by the number of people, and the diversity, and the way no one seemed bothered by each other. They appeared very different but also very alike, joined by a common factor that brought them together.

People started coming over to Christian and greeting him and his friends. Susan was the only familiar face there. She greeted them warmly before moving on to other responsibilities. The guys responded to the warm welcome with smiles. They had only been inside for three minutes and were already enjoying themselves. Hip hop music with rhymes laid over a tight drum n' bass beat blared from the speakers invisible to the naked eyes. They made their way over to the counter to collect their bowling shoes.

AJ was intrigued. People were having fun, bowling, laughing, eating pizza and socializing. There was nothing vulgar coming out of their mouths, no cursing, no swearing. The girls seemed relaxed and smiley. He wanted to talk to them all, but he wanted to show respect too and tried really hard not to stare. He felt… at home. The song changed and a huge roar filled the atmosphere. AJ listened closely and realized that the songs were gospel.

"Hi everyone, we are so happy you made it! Are you enjoying yourselves?"

A middle-aged man dressed like a hobo is speaking over the music as he got ready to roll a ball down the corridor towards three remaining pins.

"That's my pastor," Christian said.

The crowd was clapping and cheering.

"We are here to enjoy some good Gospel Hip Hop while I teach you people how to make a strike."

Laughter erupted. Pastor rolled the ball, and it slipped into the gutter. More laughter. Even AJ and Isaac were now laughing.

"He is still warming up."

First Lady was almost the same age as Pastor but looked far younger. Her grace and the glitter in her eyes made those who encountered her feel loved and appreciated.

"Please remember that while we are here to have fun, we are also available for anyone who wants to talk or needs prayer."

"And welcome to all the new people," Pastor quipped in, as he prepared to release another gutter ball.

Colton had his shades on, covering his eyes so his opponents couldn't read his face. There were a few tables playing, and this was a little bigger than he thought. A big guy approached the table with a basket. "Cell phones, guys." They all put their phones in, and Devin held his breath. He wasn't expecting that.

The shuffling and dealing began, and Devin looked around. One of the dudes at the table frowned and said,

"Colton, next time leave your shifty friends at home. Hey kid, this is a fast table, you're holding us up!"

Devin folded and started tapping his foot. Out of nowhere there was a knock at the front door. The big guy looked out, and the door blew open. Guys with covered faces and guns in their hands charged in. "Get down on the ground, GET DOWN." They yelled it over and over. Everyone hit the ground, Devin's face next to Colton's. Colton looked terrified, breathing hard. Money was grabbed off the tables, and one of the older guys stood up. A member of the gang started screaming in his face, "Better get down, old man. Don't be playin' no hero."

The old man had strong arms and a broad chest and didn't look easily intimidated. He moved to push the guy out of the way and took the butt of the gun in his face. Blood poured from his nose. He dropped to the ground, and Colton realized he was unconscious. He started fumbling for his phone to call for help, but remembered they were still locked up.

The gang got called off by the leader, and they all ran out. No one could see their faces. Devin stood up at once. "I want out of here, man, give me my phone." The big guy threw down the basket and everyone grabbed their phones. Colton scrambled to the man on the floor to check if he was still breathing. He had seen stuff like this in video games, but that was scary. Real life had outdone the virtual reality he was so used to every day, and it was not cool. His palms were sweaty, and his heart hammered against his ribs, hands shaking as he dialed 911.

An ambulance showed up eventually. Colton broke down as he walked home, feeling like eyes were following him all the way. Once the adrenaline dropped, the fear took over. He couldn't stop crying, and everything shaked. His knees were weak, and he wanted to run all the way home, but he couldn't. He wondered what happened to Devin. He must have been as terrified as Colton, and that was why he bolted.

§

The free pizzas and drink were all gone, and some people are getting fidgety and impatient. Pastor signaled for the DJ to turn the music down.

"I know how it is when the food's all gone. You guys gonna start filing out secretly behind our backs. Before you do, the First Lady wants to take care of some business." Pastor glanced up at his board. First Lady was registering more strikes than him. He smiled at her embarrassingly as she took his place.

"I know God is speaking to some hearts tonight. It might be yours, or the person next to you. God is pulling at you because the image and inscription of God is engraved in our inner consciousness. God knew you before He formed you in your mother's womb. Every human life is equally valued and represented in Jesus Christ. You are the expression of the greatest idea that ever was. God wrote the script of your DNA when He knitted you together in your mother's womb, the code is 'Christ in you!' If you feel there is a void within you, this message is for you. You have tried everything you could just to feel better for a moment, and then you feel the big hole again. Jesus wants you to know that He is in you. The mystery that was hidden for ages and generations is now revealed: It is Christ in you. Jesus is not hiding in history or in the future, or in outer space; He is "I am" in you! There is nothing wrong with your design or your redemption. Our thoughts have gone astray, but His hasn't. Remember, Jesus, the Shepherd never forsook the sheep. Knowing Jesus Christ will set you free from the feeling of lacking something you can't explain, the feeling of being void or empty."

Isaac and AJ felt the sting of her words simultaneously. Her voice had an inviting tone, very hard to ignore. They were both amazed and worried at how precise she was in the comment about the void. Isaac wondered if Christian said something about their conversations on the emptiness. *Why else would she say that?* Isaac was aware of the unease creeping in, and he was no longer enjoying himself. He was struggling between the vulnerability of a profound feeling in front of a stranger. First Lady signaled the DJ for a song but playing low. The bass started thumping, and Isaac breathed out, putting the thoughts from his mind, and letting peace settle back in. The drumbeat followed and suddenly, he was into the groove. *How can this feel so perfect?* His ears tuned into the lyrics, and he heard the coolest rapper telling him to dream again, that God's love had always been there with him, even when he fell. The chorus of the song really resonated with him, and the smile that had gone once more blossomed on his face. He looked over to see what AJ might be thinking and saw him sitting with his head in his hands. "You okay, man?"

AJ looked up and Isaac could see tears running down his face. "Like, dude, what is wrong with me?" And despite the tears, he laughed. It was so weird to him. Isaac may be holding back the way he felt, but something inside AJ was breaking – and yet he felt whole. It was a feeling he had never experienced before, and he definitely needed some clarity on it.

Christian sat down next to them, and he answered AJ's question. "It is a beautiful experience, isn't it, to feel God?" Christian spoke with a huge smile, feeling the joy of AJ's awareness. He put a hand on his shoulder and tried to make him understand that everything was going to be all right, even better than before.

The song continued to play as Pastor gave an invitation, "If you haven't personally experienced the Lordship of Jesus, and you would like to partake of the amazing Life in you, come closer. We would love to pray with you."

The lights continued to flicker, changing hues and colors randomly. It seemed almost as if it was dancing to the music playing softly in the background. AJ had never experienced such a perfect blend of sight, sound and emotions. Isaac sat back and watched as AJ went closer for prayer. Isaac could see AJ, his shoulders shaking a little. Christian moved next to Isaac. "What did you think?"

"It was nice." Isaac wanted to just give in, but there was a part of him that was still skeptical. His head would not allow him to accept something he did not fully understand yet, but he could definitely sense a presence in the room he had never felt before.

Christian wanted Isaac to enjoy his evening and have fun meeting the other members of the church. He wanted him to enjoy it as a lifestyle, as well as an event.

AJ walked back towards them, and he was grinning from ear to ear. He gave Christian a hug. "Man, I have never felt so good in my entire life." He started to choke up again. "I feel like I could put up with anything and still be happy, as long as this feeling inside lasts."

Christian laughed. The atmosphere was happy and calm, with people cheering each other on.

When AJ got home, nothing had changed. Dinner was cold as usual; his mom was passed out on the couch with a toppled bottle of prescription drugs by her hand. At first, he thought she was dead, until he noticed the heaving of her chest going up and down and the subtle waves of the sea trying to encroach beyond its borders. He then felt a smack in the back of his head, and a crusty, half-sober voice followed, "Boy, get me a beer, will ya."

"Sure, dad."

AJ went to the kitchen and took a beer out of the fridge. He popped the cover off, his eyes glanced on a bottle of cyanide sitting on top of the kitchen counter as if someone deliberately put it there for him to see. The thought of being free from his abusive father crept into his thoughts. *Just one drop several times a day should shut the human body down eventually. It would be seen as a natural death. No one would ever know.* AJ was very familiar with this train of thought, but now there was something different. Another voice, saying something else. There is a way that seems right to a man, but the end is death.

AJ took the beer to his father, who half emptied the bottle in one go.

"Where are you coming from at this hour, boy?"

"I was just hanging with the boys." AJ responded, half prepared to defend himself against any repercussions.

"It's not safe for you to be on the streets at this hour. If something happened to you, who would fetch my beers and buy my cigarettes."

"Is that all I'm good for to you," AJ thought. *You know better than to allow such thoughts to become words.*

His father pointed at his mother, "Look at this old witch. She takes pain meds like water. Them poison gonna kill her one of these days. I'm just so sick and tired of this house…of her…of you." He finished the beer. AJ said nothing.

"You just gonna stand there like a darn statute. Get me another beer."

This time AJ took the bottle of cyanide and put it where it was supposed to be. He did an inward inspection as he opened another bottle of beer. The peace he experienced just moments before was still there. He smiled.

Devin laughed with his gang buddies as they threw back shots of vodka. He was officially in the gang now. "Can you believe they took our phones? Good thing I popped that text off first!" The laughter rose, and Devin felt like a king. Now he was part of the group, he could start making money. He already got his cut for the night and knew what he was gonna do with it— new kicks, and some new clothes. He was going to start looking like the king he was, and he had no intention of stopping there. He was gonna go all the way to the top.

CHAPTER SEVEN

ncle Jim was out shopping at the mall with Simone. They were going from store to store, looking at different apparels, jewelry, and testing perfumes. Jim did his best to meet the demands of his young girlfriend, but it got overwhelming sometimes trying to balance his own responsibilities and keeping her in check. She was wild at heart and really just needed someone she could depend on to meet her needs. He used her as a cover up for his alter ego; the other version of himself that was drawn to young boys. It was a struggle he developed long after being sexually abused himself by a minister at the church his mom frequented. No one believed him when he cried for help, so he went inside himself and stayed there locked away behind distant memories and his own perverted mind.

Simone was a little bit too clingy for his taste, but she was good company and an effective distraction. She kept him occupied enough that he didn't notice Dominic following them from a safe distant, his face hidden in the shadow of the hood that was pulled over his face. Jim didn't see Dom or the tip of the nine-inch blade sticking out of his back pocket.

§

AJ woke up from a beautiful dream. He and his friends were all decked in white and attending a wedding. There was a belief that dreaming about a wedding was preparing for a funeral. AJ was not sure if he should interpret the dream literally, but he was still reeling from the emotions he felt in the dream. His newfound path really made him feel different --- new. His parents were skeptical at first, but they have been warming up more to his apparent changes when they noticed him smiling more. His mannerisms had improved, and he was more open to the plans they had for him.

§

Jim excused himself to take a bathroom break. Simone teased that she would join him, which he tactfully declined and disappeared down a passageway leading to the restroom. Dominic followed.

Jim was paying no attention to the door opening and the hooded man that walked in. Dominic was clutching the blade of the knife as he stepped into one of the toilet booth. He had been trying to convince himself for the past hour that he was capable of doing this; that Uncle Jim deserved to have his life taken from him for what he did. The young Dom within was crying out for vengeance. He wanted this pervert to pay for the scars he had inflicted on at least two lives. Dom didn't know his past, nor cared to know. Jim was given the responsibility to watch over them, not take advantage of them; not seek to satisfy some misguided desire to rob two boys of their innocence and thwart their promising future with the struggles that would ensue from such acts.

Dominic heard the sound of the soap dispensing, and the swooshing of water over dirty hands. He knew he had but a fraction of a second to determine if he was going to go through with it. He wanted to so badly, but there was something else screaming inside him, something that prevented his feet from shifting, his hands from releasing him out of that cubicle. Dominic realized that all it took was one moment to change the trajectory of one's life and in that moment, he made a choice that would have serious implications on his life.

AJ was attending church with Christian. elated to be spending time with his friend, but also with his new best friend, Jesus. He had never experienced anything like this before. The more he prayed and read his Bible, the more he stopped believing that church was boring. He started seeing it as somewhere believers came together in fellowship with one another, and fellowship with God through the Word. His relationship with his Savior became so much more real and fun now that he was talking to Jesus everywhere and any time.

Colton called to ask for a quick meet up with Christian. AJ was there with him. When Colton showed up, it was clear that he was annoyed to see AJ there, but he didn't say anything. He was uneasy, unsure how they would take the news of the poker game. It was too much, too scary. He knew he had to get out of that life before something worse happened.

Colton told them what went down, and Christian had some things to say that AJ found shocking.

"That's what happens when you're addicted to what isn't part of your original nature, man." Christian shaked his head sadly.

"Hey Christian, can I be saved from this sin?" Colton was afraid of what could happen to him.

"There can be no salvation from something, if the thing we need saving from causes the only qualified Savior to squeamishly tuck tail and run away. If sin had the power to separate man from God, God would lack the power to separate man from sin. Therefore, the only possibility for salvation is that God must be able to sit right there with us in fellowship, even in our darkest moments and biggest messes." Christian looked disappointed, but not angry. He knew very well that the path of sin led to suffering and death. He had seen it happen before and it was not something he desired for his friends.

Colton broke down, crying into his hands. "It was really scary, man. These guys were going to kill us, and I can't deal with stuff like that. I need to change man, my life sucks!"

Christian nodded. "The arms of God are opened far wider than our narrow minds will ever be able to fully grasp. The most amazing thing about Jesus is that no matter what we do or go through, whenever we are ready, He has His arms wide open for a big hug. I think after something like that, you should talk to an adult. Pastor is really good at making time for people."

"I will go see him," Colton said wiping his face, feeling better for making the commitment to try it. "But honestly, what does that do for me? How do I fix my life? I still want to gamble. I just want to know that the next time I am safe, and that security is gone. I knew all of those guys. No one should have known about that game."

Christian replied in a very calm tone, "There was a time when I was clearly obsessed with sin or what I considered sin, though you would have never thought so by the way I talked. I was very much anti-sin, and yet I was obsessed with it. It was all I talked about and all I thought about. Everyone I used to talk with; you guys and anyone else, it was about how to live above sin or how to be free from certain sinful vices, and yet, in my attempts at freedom from sin, I only showed how obsessed with, and entangled in it I was. Now, I don't mean that I was out doing the very things I was railing against. I only mean that, while I once indulged in certain behaviors, now I ranted against them with as much passion as I once indulged in them, and, in so doing, revealed that, while I had switched teams, I was still enslaved. Sin still haunted my thoughts, and I was as much its servant as ever. Freedom is not manifested in a hatred for a thing, nor as a protest against it, as that really only goes to show that you still love it, but feel guilty for doing so, and so overcompensate by constantly speaking out against it. Real freedom is manifested when the thing no longer has its hooks in your mind in any way, shape or form. Your protests aren't ways of masking your desire for it, but come from a place of deep love, and true concern for people's wellbeing. You do not, however, fearfully obsess over becoming entangled in a behavior, nor feel the need to vicariously chide yourself by constantly chiding others. Surprisingly, freedom actually feels like freedom. It isn't a matter of exchanging chains for handcuffs, or a prison cell in Alcatraz for one in Guantanamo. It looks like being unshackled, both inwardly and outwardly. A healthy mind isn't one whose obsessions point left, whereas they used to point right, but a mind no longer obsessed. So let me say this very simply: an obsession with being holy is no less enslaving than an obsession with sin. It is the exact same unhealthy obsession, just bent in the opposite direction. You know the things you are doing on impulse or feel like you can't live without, addiction… Those things are meant to satisfy the feeling of lacking something you don't know you're missing. We can ask anyone and see what they have struggled with…watch this…" Christian looked around and noticed a man walking towards them on his phone. He smiled politely, and said, "Excuse me sir… Sir?"

The man looked at Christian and answered kindly. "Yes, young man?"

"May we ask you a question?"

The man looked the boys over. "Sure, what do you want to know?"

"We were just wondering - have you ever struggled with something you had to do, but didn't want to?"

The man was well-dressed in a three-piece suit. His phone was expensive, the newest on the market. He smiled, pleased with himself for helping the next generation - and in a way, he was. "Yes, sure. In my work. I hustle day in and day out to make sure I have the money I need to buy the things I want. My struggle was with making compulsive decisions without initial thought. I was addicted to it actually. Does that answer your question?"

"Yes, sir. Thank you."

The man continued walking, going back to the phone conversation Christian pulled him from, nodding at the guys as he went.

Colton was excited by that answer. "That's what I'm trying to do!"

Christian shaked his head. "There's a personal choice to make every time you have a thought. If you do stuff you can't get rid of, it's a form of idolatry, which means you're engaged with a distorted image of yourself. It means you are obsessed with something you feel you must have in order to complete you."

"So if I start knowing Jesus, I will never be able to choose anything in this world again?" Colton was troubled with this thought. What Christian presented as a great argument seemed completely wrong for him.

Christian shaked his head again trying to find a clear way to get his point across, "Eve had a choice in the garden when she was tempted to eat from the forbidden tree. God always knows what's best for you. If you talk to Him to find out what His plan for your life is, you won't be living a life you're not supposed to live. Because He loves you, He will tell you or reveal to you what you need to know."

Colton laughed. "Bruh, I am not too familiar with the Eve-story. What I know is that she could have eaten from any other tree, but I'm not sure why she felt like she lacked something. I was told they had everything they could think of in that place. But maybe I would have done the same in her position, who knows."

AJ was watching. He was anxious to share his amazing testimony, but he had so much to learn. He had been texting Isaac, who wanted to meet up. AJ imagined he must feel the change too, the emptiness melting away as God's love overwhelmed him. AJ loved God now and felt love for everyone. God's love was bringing security and fulfillment to his heart and mind.

Christian wanted to help Colton's understanding of Christianity so he might join them. "For many of those who are lost, a fun church may seem like an oxymoron."

Colton jumped in again. "Church, fun? Really? I honestly don't think so."

"You're right, bruh. I used to wonder the same thing, and some of us were taken to traditional churches in our entire childhood. Today I have a better understanding of what it is; the Ekklesia is the visible expression of God with Jesus as the head."

"Oh, for real? So, people don't need to go to church? They don't need a physical gathering with other believers to hear the Word of God?"

Christian jumped in, "We definitely need to go, that's why I go now - but with a better understanding of why I am attending meetings or special events."

Colton bit his lips, taking a moment, "Okay…so why do people go to services every week?"

Christian started smiling. He was happy his friend was trying to understand why it was important to go to a local church. It was clear that Colton wanted to get it.

"Here are a couple of reasons why you should go. Some are serious and thought provoking, others are just fun. The Bible says we should not forsake the assembling of ourselves together. It's an opportunity to worship God with others, and you will get some of life's big questions answered. You will make new friends, get encouragement to stay the course, meet your soul mate."

"I like that one," Colton said, smiling.

"Church helps us understand what the Bible is all about. We are taught the value of God, others and ourselves. And, people who attend church live longer."

"Are you serious?"

"I didn't make that up. Ask Dr. Google."

"Go on," Colton said.

"Attending church facilitates your development as a leader. We can get help when we need it and experience other people's love. It's an opportunity to demonstrate love. Hearing what God is doing in and through other believers can unveil the faith in you. We receive prayer; see our prayers answered and share what God is doing for us. Coming together also honors and glorifies God and we will be taken to the journey of discovering the realities of who Jesus is and who we are in Him. We learn to set our priorities right, focus on God and on His creation, find strength for our self-faith, improve self-esteem and interpersonal skills and learn to cope with the difficulties in life."

"It all sounds good," Colton said, still looking and feeling unsure.

"Church is a reminder that we are not alone. We get help with shaping our vision for the future, and encourages creativity. We feel closer to God, though we can't really get closer because we are already one with Him. We will discover the natural gifts and talents that we have in us, but above all, attending church can help to keep us out of trouble."

AJ finally spoke to top it all off, "You would be crazy not to go to church with all those reasons." AJ shared how his experience at the bowling alley had changed his perception of life. He no longer saw life and people through eyes of skepticism, uncertainty and dislike. He realized that even the behavior of his parents was a result of their enslavement to a depraved mental perception. They really had no idea what they were doing or how it affected the people around them. AJ finally saw that love became a choice and it was not based on whether the recipient deserved it or not.

The wisdom of God through Christian was simply amazing. He was as passionate as he was knowledgeable, and his voice was inviting but still soft and firm. The gospel had opened his eyes, and he had lost all fear of speaking about the heart of the Lord freely to his friends.

He looked back at Colton openly, hiding nothing. Then added, "You know what, bruh?"

Colton was disarmed in the face of this wisdom, and said, "Tell me."

"Local churches should be vibrant and exciting gatherings where lovers meet their Lover. Church is God's idea. It is a dynamic and loving family coming together to love on Father, Son and Holy Spirit, and be enlightened. When anyone goes to church, they should expect to grow in their understanding and awareness of their eternal identity in Christ. When you grow in understanding and consciousness, what has been true about you in Christ Jesus, then God's wisdom is exhibited through your words and actions. We're all brothers and sisters in the heart of Jesus Christ and He wants us to love and accept each other regardless of mundane differences."

AJ understood it. Colton started getting it. "That sounds great and it looks like a fun place. When I was little, I saw people walking by looking happy to go to church. They'd come out with an even bigger smile, and I always believed church must be the most fun place on the planet, especially on a Sunday morning. It was something I used to think about a lot and always felt the same way about it, deep down. But then it started to seem boring for some reason, I still don't know why."

Christian was smiling and thanked God in his heart. *"Thank you, Father of our Lord Jesus Christ, for starting to open to eyes of my friend, Colton."*

"I need to know something. Sometimes I find myself dwelling on doubting thoughts and I don't know sometimes where these kinds of thoughts come from. Can you please help me with that? Does that happen to you sometimes; to doubt?" Colton was being honest about himself.

"Sure, I'm a very good doubter too. Jesus is the very good believer. So, we don't get too hung up on our inability to reconcile this with that or that with this. We are not required to try hard to believe anything. We are all invited to rest in the fact that Christ believes, and Christ was faithful as me, not just for me. Therefore, we can sit here with our doubts, questions, and inability to reconcile A with B, and be perfectly at peace, knowing that we are as safe and secure as the eternal Son of the heavenly Father is, Himself."

"Wonderfully said," Colton had given Christian his attention.

"But you know what? Church is not just on Sunday. As sons of God we're supposed to have fun every single day and everywhere we find ourselves. The Bible is like a roadmap sometimes. It teaches us what is right and what is wrong, and above all things it reveals life in us. Once we start to participate in the relationship between Jesus and His Father, the ability to live the Christ-life will be possible by the assistance of Holy Spirit in us. We'll speak to people the way Jesus speaks to people, we'll love the way He loves, we'll forgive the way He forgives; you get the idea. The goodness of humanity doesn't draw out the love of God, rather, it is the love of God that draws out the inherent goodness of humanity."

"It doesn't seem so hard, so why do people find it difficult?" Colton was sincere when he asked this. He was not thinking about it, just opening his mouth, and letting the words come out. Christian had created a trust atmosphere in which his friends felt like they could ask him anything. They won't be judged and would get an honest answer in return.

Christian continued in the same inviting tone, "The relationship with Jesus is not something a disembodied spirit named 'God' began to pine for during that long period prior to creation, and we are not the robots He fashioned to scratch that relational itch. Neither is relationship a sort of epiphenomenon that God stumbled upon after the act of creation. Relationship, family, and community are at the very core of the nature of God. He does not create family, but is family, eternally. The Father, Son and Spirit know one another from everlasting to everlasting, and God created, not so that He may be known, and have both His ego stroked and His desire for companionship satisfied, but so that others may encounter the joy of being known, just as the Godhead knows one another. In fact, according to the words of Brother Paul, any knowledge of God that we may have is a result of God's knowledge of us. This is how we know: by encountering the reality that we are known. You were not created to complete God. He is complete. You were created that you might be a sharer in the completeness that comes from being completely known, and completely loved, because it is a relationship, not a set of rules. God hears me when I talk to Him, so I pray as often as I can - not to ask for things, but to thank Him for what He has already done for me. God will never let you go. You are His beloved so receiving His love and participating in His life every single day becomes part of you. Knowing the unchanging, unconditional and immeasurable love of God is the sure antidote to any sense of lack and void. He makes everything complete in every way which can be found so there's no emptiness for those who are in Christ, for Christ is ALL in them."

Isaac appeared on the other side of the street, and AJ waved him over. He had texted that he had something important to talk about. Colton and Christian stopped talking to greet him.

"Hey guys. I'm having a pool party later. It'll just be our crew. I need to tell you all something."

"You getting married, man?" asked Colton with a grin.

"Yeah, man!" Isaac cracked up. "C'mon, you know better! I just need to talk to all my friends at once."

"Did you get a hold of everyone else?" Christian liked to make sure that if anyone said everyone, it meant everyone.

"I sent texts. No one really responded."

"I didn't get one," Christian took his phone out of his pocket and looked at it.

"I did, you just didn't see it yet."

"Good call, it's there in the group chat. What time?" Christian asked.

"Be there at four. I have some things to grab. I'll see you later." Isaac took off towards the store, keys jingling in his hands. He always rode his bike with the guys or walked with them. He had an expensive Mercedes his parents gave him, but he never liked to drive it when he was with his friend. It did not have enough seats for everyone, so he only drove when he was alone. Every now and then he would take one or a few of them farther than their little town, but he seemed embarrassed about his parent's extravagance. He just wanted to be one of the crew.

AJ piped up. "It is getting a little late. We should probably go."

The guys separated, wondering what this impromptu announcement could be. Isaac had seemed distant, bothered almost. His family pool was amazing though! The guys were always hoping for an invitation to come and swim at the house. The pool was large with slides going into the deep end, and diving boards. There was a pool house with a hangout center, life jackets, floaties, and a climbing wall they could jump from into the water. All the guys looked forward to hanging for the evening. Isaac was the only one who was not excited. He knew everyone was going to be disappointed with the news.

§

Dominic walked briskly towards the exit of the Mall, bumping into a few people as he chose not to detour from his desired destination. He wanted to be far away from that place as quickly as his feet could take him.

"Dom," A familiar female voice reverberated in Dom's ears, stopping him in his tracks. He was walking so fast, he didn't notice Mitch beckoning in his direction.

"Dom, are you okay? We haven't seen you in a couple days." Mitch's voice was usually littered with sentimentality and concern, even though she acted and dressed like a man most of the time.

"I --- had some family issues to deal with."

"Don't we all. We always still try to stick together, but I'm starting to feel like our circle is falling apart."

"It is what it is, Mitch."

"You saw the text from Isaac?"

"Yeah. I did."

"Let's try to be there, huh. This could be good for us…all of us."

Dominic glanced past Mitch to see Uncle Jim coming towards them with Simone clutching gingerly to his arms.

They were pointing and laughing like two teenagers in love.

"I gotta go. See you later."

Dominic didn't wait for Mitch to respond. Her eyebrows were knitted with concern. She knew that everyone had their own darkness within and she couldn't help but feel that something traumatic was about to tear her little crew apart.

CHAPTER EIGHT

The afternoon hours dragged on slowly as the guys waited to go to Isaac's. It seemed like an eternity for them, but for Isaac it felt like only seconds. At four PM, everyone started tapering in. A text message came in the group that Dominic was not going to make it. Devin and Mitch were the last to show up. Once Devin arrived, they started racing through the house to the pool and goofing off.

Isaac didn't have the resolve to wait until the end of their fun-time to make his announcement. He stood up to get it out of the way, "Hey, guys, I'm gonna say this real quick. My parents are going to Europe for the rest of the summer."

Will said, "Oh, good for them."

Isaac gave him a look. "Dude, they're making me go too."

AJ raised both his arms. "That's awesome! You'll get to see a bunch of amazing things and make memories."

Exasperation set in, and Isaac felt his cheeks getting hot. "Thanks, I guess. But I hate that we're leaving! I wanted to have fun with you guys this summer, because life sends us in different directions every year, and this was like the last summer for fun, ya know? I don't really want to go."

"Okay, sure, but you got a chance to see the world. This place never changes. You'll be back and we will still be here to have fun with." Thomas didn't speak often, but when he did, the guys listened.

"I know you're right. You are. It´s just that I feel I would be missing lots of things while I'm away and that's never cool. But let's just wait and see… you're right. Let's have a good night." Isaac cannonballed into the pool, glad to have that over with.

"Where's Mitch," Devin asked, finally noticing that she was nowhere in sight.

Thomas was the first to see her walk out of the changing room wearing a two-piece bath suit. His mouth was wide open, and he was shocked into silence. All the other eyes turned to see what he was looking at, and they were all smitten. They had never seen Mitch dressed like a lady, let alone in a bath suit. Her curvature was perfect, and her walk was slightly lacking the tomboy grace that they were used to.

"What!" Mitch said, averting the attention of all the eyes looking at her, "I know you've all seen a girl in bath suit before." Christian had been trying hard not to gaze. Devin noticed and points in his direction mockingly.

"Mitch, you better cover up before the holy man sins himself."

Mitch dived into the pool. Christian seemed a bit relieved.

"And you'll need to stop looking at my sister like she some kinda stranger."

§

All the guys were out of the pool, dressed and gathered around a fire pit roasting hot dogs, bread, kebabs and mushrooms, to say the least. AJ decided to make use of the opportunity to share his good news with all the guys before Isaac went missing. It blurted out of him, because he just couldn't keep it in. "Something happened to me the other night at the bowling alley. I realized that Jesus loved me, and I agreed to live with Him for the rest of my life!"

He reeled back as a half-roasted mushroom slammed him in the face. "Oh, sorry man." Devin's voice was dark, and his apology flat.

AJ blinked, his face stinging. "You did that on purpose, dude, that's not cool…" His voice trailed off. He realized that a few weeks ago he would have wanted to fight, but now he was calm. He was hurt, but calm. It flooded him with shame that he used to treat Christian like that too, so he lets it go. It won't do any good to get mad.

Colton changed the subject quickly, because he didn't want anyone fighting tonight. "Dev, I haven't heard from you. What did you think about what happened the other night?"

"What happened?" Will jumped in, because he knew Colton was talking about the poker game, and he was the one originally asked to go.

"Some armed robbers showed up and wiped out all the money." Colton knew it looked bad, but it *was* bad.

"Dang! I'm glad I didn't go!"

Devin had a weird look on his face. "That was something else. Your boy gonna make it up to us?"

"Nah, bruh, they didn't. He lost the most though, so I doubt he'll be hosting another game or coming to any for a long time." Colton felt bad for the brave older guy who stood up trying to stop the robbers. He got a nasty cut where the butt of the gun smacked his face.

"There any rumors about who did it?" Devin was careful to appear nonchalant about what might be circulating.

"Nah, nothing. No one knew about that game except the people in the room, and everybody got robbed…so it must have been a coincidence, or someone messed up." Colton had been trying to make sense of the whole thing, but there were no answers.

Thomas couldn't help himself. "That's messed up! You gonna keep gambling, Colton?"

"Probably not. I'm going to church with Christian and AJ on Sunday."

Another mushroom went flying out of nowhere and bounced off Christian's head. He laughed, grabbed it, and ate it. "When will you be leaving, Isaac?"

"Two days. What's up with your church, dude? Everybody's starting to go. Must be a pretty chill place." Although Isaac already made it clear he had looked at a few religions, the changes in his friends were hard to deny. He was so sure he had it figured out, but that idea was crumbling little by little. But it didn't matter. His parents wouldn't accept him changing to be a part of Christianity. They didn't want him to even entertain the idea of visiting a church. They already had plans for him to see a psychiatrist because he went to the bowling alley with church folks. They believed Christianity was a mindless religion devoid of free will and intellectual flexibility.

Christian grinned. "It's a fun place to be at. You can meet new people; people come from other cities to our amazing youth gatherings. Most importantly though, is that the Spirit of the Lord engineers these radical transformations. We are led from an inferior mindset to the revealed knowledge of our authentic identity. Pastor James and his wife doesn't speak to us to make us feel good, they minister to us from God's heart – I believe they desire for us to understand that we are no longer slaves to fear, rather we are sons and daughters of God, and we are profoundly loved by Him. That helps us enjoy a real and authentic relationship with Jesus, which also helps us to truly experience the extremities of God's love and kindness in our lives. Dude, you should come."

Devin was getting more and more fidgety by the second.

"I'm leaving Saturday, so I won't be able to. Maybe when we get back. No promises though." Isaac said.

Mitch looked at AJ and asked, "AJ, does the emptiness really go? You seem different, but I can't tell what's changed just by looking at you."

AJ nodded, looking happy. "It really does. I'm still working on all the answers though. Man, you know my parents—the Drunk and the Pill Popper. My dad drinks and does horrible stuff to my mom, and she stays high so he can't hurt her anymore. I started to sneak alcohol and drugs. I wanted everything to disappear so I could escape the fighting. I thought I was stuck in the same trap that they were—working factory jobs that barely pay the bills, living paycheck to paycheck, no chance of doing better…but now, I find hope in Jesus Christ. I now pray for my family and no matter what I see, I believe God has a bright plan for our lives. When I heard that Jesus died for me, all I could think of was that I wasn't worth that, and then it hit me that He found me worthy… I believe that my parents were included in God's mind when Jesus died for all men and women." AJ choked a little. "Me…worthy. The emptiness ceased to be immediately, but I am still learning, and the Word of God is having an impact in my heart and mind every day."

Another mushroom whizzed through the air and slammed Will square in the face. Will recovered and yelled, "DEVIN—you're a jerk! What's your problem? You aren't even fun anymore. You're just mean!"

Devin finally got to his feet and started yelling at the guys, "I hate all of you! You dig it? Bunch of weak chumps. My new friends are way chill, not standing around talking about fairytale pretend bologna, but real life—clubs, women, sex, making money, hanging out and having fun…You turds want to talk about things like this and make yourselves sound better than everybody else. Face this fact - you are *not* better than anybody else. You're boring, lame and childish! I'm through wasting my time hanging around you. I'm done hearing about your imaginary friends." Devin grabbed his T-shirt off a chair and slipped his shoes on. He grabbed his phone and some food, and went through the fence door, throwing up his middle fingers as a parting shot. "See ya, losers!" No one attempted to go after him. Will glanced at Mitch.

"Is he in a gang now?" Will was still mad. "I hope he stays gone."

"He's still my brother," Mitch said defensively.

"And he's still our friend," Christian confirmed.

Isaac was watching Devin walk away, "I don't know…but he's really changed."

Thomas was really bothered by this row with his old pal. These guys had been together for a long time, and they had all changed as they have grown, but Devin had become violent and had been making scary decisions. This gang was no joke. They were known for being involved with drugs, rape, arson, vandalism, theft, and even some convicted murders, as well as rumored ones. All the guys knew that nobody felt the sting of his change more than Mitch. She managed to remain cool because all her attempts to reach her brother had backfired on her, violently.

It was a lot to take in for Thomas. His parents were still married. They worked and stayed out of trouble, but they yelled at each other and their kids. His parents whup them sometimes, and there may have been a few discipline sessions that have gone too far, but he wouldn't say they were abusive. There was no love either, but family meals at the table - even if most were in silence - are a daily occurrence, and they made sure needs were met—clothes, food, shelter, all of it.

Devin, on the other hand, had lost his dad in prison to violence. All the guys loved his mother, who worked multiple jobs to provide for her children. Her name was Grace, and she seemed full of it. She was always tired when the guys saw her, but she would still flash her pearly grin and talk to them for a few minutes. She taught her kids well when she was around, and Thomas was sure she had no clue what her oldest son was up to. He wanted to tell her somehow to save Devin, but he was too afraid it would backfire.

Colton interrupted everyone's thoughts, "This ain't about Devin. Isaac invited us here to have fun! Let's do it! He'll be gone in a few days so let's make his mini party a blast."

Christian piped up, "Can we put some background music on? I got the hip-hop CD that they were playing songs from at the bowling alley the other night."

"You guys will love it!" AJ was visibly excited, bouncing up and down.

Isaac nodded. "It was cool, you guys will like it."

"The CD's on the table with the snacks." Christian gestured towards the table. Devin's leaving put a damper on the party, but in some ways, it was a good thing. Now they could talk without him interrupting with his attitude.

§

The night was winding down, the food was all gone, the music was playing softly in the background. Mitch was glaring up at the stars, while AJ and Thomas were clearing up plates and putting things back the way they should be.

Will had a curious look on his face as he turned to Christian, "Look, I know I say things sometimes, but I need to know…how can you be sure the things you say are real? You can't see Jesus so what if you are just wasting your time and life on something that doesn't exist? How do you even know He died for us?"

Christian answered first, "While billions of people believe Jesus was one of the most important figures in world history, many others reject the idea that He even existed at all. The first-century Jewish historian Flavius Josephus, who according to Ehrman 'is far and away our best source of information about first-century Palestine,' twice mentions Jesus in *Jewish Antiquities*, in 93 A.D when he wrote on the history of the Jewish people. He was born a few years after the crucifixion of Jesus around 37 A.D., Josephus was a well-connected aristocrat and military leader in Palestine who served as a commander in Galilee during the first Jewish Revolt against Rome between 66 and 70 A.D. Although Josephus was not a follower of Jesus, 'he was around when the early church was getting started,' so he knew people who had seen and heard Jesus. Somewhere in Jewish *Antiquities* there is a recount of an unlawful execution, Josephus identifies the victim, James, as the 'brother of Jesus-who-is-called-Messiah.' More debate surrounds Josephus's lengthier passage about Jesus, known as the 'Testimonium Flavianum,' which describes a man 'who did surprising deeds' and was condemned to be crucified by Pilate. So, to answer your question: yes. The crucifixion of Jesus Christ did not take place in obscurity. The writers of the four gospels were actual figures in history who wrote, from various **perspectives**, about the life, ministry, death and resurrection of Jesus of Nazareth. Their writings depicted eyewitness accounts of documented happenings in history. The variety of theories as to the events following the crucifixion and what happened to the body of Jesus, only serves to further establish the fact of this heinous death. Such well-known legends as the swoon theory, that Jesus only passed out on the cross and was later resuscitated by the cool air of the tomb, and the case of the stolen body are strewn throughout literature chronicling the events of that time. The fact is, the *death* of Jesus Christ was *never* disputed. The Jews, both those who hated him and those who would become His future followers, witnessed His death. It was a public event. Jesus said, *'But I, when I am lifted up from the earth, will draw all men to myself.'* This was an announcement of the success of his agenda to redeem and save all men. Remember, God reconciled all men to Himself in Jesus. Joseph of Arimathea, himself a notable figure of the Jews of that day, requested the body of Jesus in order to give Him an honorable burial. As to the validity of the mode of execution, it was established that by the first century, crucifixion was the Roman method for certain non-Roman criminals. It was initially employed as a form of punishment causing extreme pain and humiliation, so much so that the word 'excruciating' was created for the express purpose of describing the unfathomable horror of the individual's suffering on a cross. Excruciating literally means, *'out of the cross.'* If a man guilty of a capital offense is put to death and his body is hung on a tree, you must not leave his body on the tree overnight. Be sure to bury him that same day, because anyone who is hung on a tree is under God's curse."

"Alright, so, why all the misconceptions about God, religion and us?" Everyone was looking and attentively listening to Christian, Will seemed to have more questions for Christian.

"Religion thrives on two lies: distance and delay. But God took the initiative to cancel every possible definition of distance or delay between Him and man. Emmanuel is introduced to a hostile humanity as the lover of their lives. Our sins couldn't distract God from His extravagant love for us. God wants us to awake and realize we can't live what He made available for us in His begotten Son, if we don't know who we are and whose we are. Ignorance will always keep us away from living the life of our design, our blessed pre-arranged life. Imagine throwing your parents away, the woman who gave birth to you. We don't do that…even people who have bad moms love them, and don't want people talking trash about them. But people talk horribly about God all the time. And you know what's crazy?"

Will was trying to wrap his head around it. He wouldn't let anyone talk about his mom. "What's crazy?"

"God keeps His arms wide open for us all, and it isn't just talk. Nothing you have done or could do will stop His love for you. His love is greater than your wrongdoing. What you think to be your worst sin or mistake is not enough to make Him walk away. Our hostility and indifference towards God did not reduce His love for us. He saw equal value in us when He exchanged the life of His Son for ours. Now that the act of reconciliation is complete, His life in us saves us from the guttermost to the uttermost. A clear and accurate understanding of the fact that God loves you will make the illusion of being empty irrelevant. When we rest in God's love in everything we do, we have rest; when we trust in that love, wherever we go, we have peace. Jesus is true life. Even if people like Devin think it's stupid, it's still true. Herein lies the secret of the power of the Gospel; there is no good news in it until the love of Father, Son, Spirit is revealed!" Christian knew the road was not always easy, but the reward was worth it.

Will looked around and realized no one was making fun anymore. "I'm gonna keep watching, man. I'm still on the fence. It can't be that easy!"

Colton chuckled. "I feel the same way, but I'm going to youth group with them to see for myself."

Mitch had been quieter than normal. "I'm in. Why don't we all just go? Who cares? We all play b-ball, we all showed up here…the bully is out, and we can fill you in, Isaac…I just think we all need to stick closer right now. We're losing everybody."

The guys all looked around at each other, and they were all nodding. Christian asked, "Anyone talked to Dom?"

"I saw him at the mall. He had a lot of his mind." Mitch said, turning her attention back to the starry night.

The guys let the talk of emptiness go that was pervasive in their group. They just goofed off, like a weight had been lifted. Christian noticed, and wondered if the other guys have. He was more confident now that every word of the gospel he shared with his friends seemed to chip away a piece of the wall that prevented them from tapping into the one source that filled us and freed us from the sense of being empty, void within or separated from God. He was careful in choosing his words. He wanted his life to be a reflection of the ideas he shared, but he was mindful that his task had become a matter of life and death. His community was changing one soul at a time. His church didn't need a corporate revival; all that was needed was for one to reach one, and the love and light would begin to spread.

The news media had been repugnant with gang related violence and death. The authorities had been investigating numerous reports of break ins, hold ups and murders with no apparent motives. No arrest had been made and no one was talking. What the news media didn't report was the involvement of Christian, AJ and other young people from the church in the community. There was no news report of the numerous times they went to clean the areas where

146

the homeless slept, or when they helped families without kids to clean their homes, wash the dishes or help the elderly take out their trash. There were no news articles published on the small programs run by these new converts that catered to different needs in the community; the soup kitchen that fed the elderly who were unable to leave their homes, and the street people who lived off the scraps from the garbage dump.

Christian could feel the cloak of darkness over their community thicken and knew it was just a matter of time before his friends were either walking in the light or consumed by the darkness, but he knew by eyes of faith that a light had been lit in his community and in the company of his friends that would only spread. He had plans to meet with AJ and the other's who may be interested in Bible Study and prayer in different areas inside and outside of the community. It was not about going to a church building anymore for impact but allowing that church where two or three are gathered to make an impact in the world.

Susan was right. Christian only needed to focus on planting seeds. The harvest was coming, and Christian was adamant that he would not leave a friend behind.

Christian went by to visit Dominic. He wasn't sure what to expect or if his friend would even receive him, but once he declared that he was not there as the friendly neighborhood preacher man, Dominic let him in. It took a while for Dominic to compose himself in order to string words into a sentence, but Christian was very patient with his friend.

"Isaac is leaving for the summer," Christian said, when he thought Dominic was ready to start talking.

"I know. He called me just before you showed up. I'm happy for him."

"Karen at work?" Christian asked, trying to keep Dominic engaged.

"Yeah. I'm on babysitting duty cause the Uncle don't come around no more."

"That's good to know."

"I wanted to kill him. Did you know that too?"

"What do you mean?"

"I followed him and his girlfriend to the mall, with a nine-inch knife in my pocket. I was gonna shove it so far inside his gut that it would come out on the other side."

"You didn't?"

"I decided against it at the last minute."

"Why?"

"Because, somehow, I could see beyond those moments. Mom would lose a brother and a son and little Marc would have nobody."

Dominic was fighting the tears that were struggling to break free.

"I realize something else. I have been in homosexual relations, which is not natural, because of what happened to me. Yet, it's not really me cause that thing is just nasty. Yet, maybe it's this void that you keep talking about, that when we allow crap in, it makes us do crappy things."

"That's another way to look at it."

"So, I'm thinking, maybe my Uncle does what he does because of something that happened when he was young. Maybe he was abused too. Maybe he's just another victim of the emptiness and if that is true, then he doesn't deserve to be murdered in a public restroom."

"You made a good choice, Dom. This is my secret to peace, joy, and fulfillment: I keep the Lord always before me. Therefore, my heart is glad always and my soul rejoices." Christian was silently breathing a sigh of relief knowing he could have lost his friend to the negative effects of the void just days prior.

"I am so angry and so bitter inside, but I ain't no murderer."

Christian was careful in choosing his words. He surmised that Dominic was pretty fragile, and it wouldn't take much to break him.

"Tomorrow is Sunday. A few of the guys want to come with me to church. It would be nice if you would join us."

Dominic was staring at his hands, thinking about what could have been. His mind was overwhelmed with so many thoughts, that he was not sure which ones belonged to him and which ones were encroaching from other sources.

"Dom.."

"Yeah, sure. I'll think about it, bruh."

§

Devin was in a boxing ring with a much bigger guy who was responsible for sending him to the hospital a few times. The gang members were always asked to prove themselves in the ring from time to time, and Devin had lost a few times to this one guy, but he never gave up. Each loss would send him reeling back to the gym in preparation for the next round as he was adamant that he would walk away a victor eventually, and the Boss would be proud.

Most of the other gang members were present, and Boss sat among them. His next-in-line whispered in his ear and lit a joint. The outcome of this match would determine if Devin qualified for the next level.

The bell chimed and the fighting began. Devin's mind was somewhat pre-occupied with his old friends. The thought of them being influenced by Christian sent an adrenaline rush through his spine and into his bloodstream. He hardly felt the first punch that landed across his face, and quickly recovered and started raining blows on his opponent. Each punch he threw was powered by the anger he felt inside, the disappointments that his childhood friends were all getting soft and judgmental. He could hear the words of his sister echoing in his mind: *"Devin, you know better. Devin this is not you. Devin, you wanna end up like dad? Is that what you really want?"* Devin was a replica of his father, but he would be better. He was better. He would never make the same mistakes his father did, and he would be responsible to take the family where dad failed to take them. Mom would not have to work so hard once he made his mark. Money would come easy. He would command the respect of everyone, and he could have any girl he wanted anytime. Girls dig a real gangster and he would stop at nothing to get to the top.

Devin's face was bloodied and bruised, but he was still standing. The other guy was lying in a bloody broken heap at his feet, groaning and unable to get up. Devin glanced over at the Boss who nodded with a pleased grin on his face. Devin would finally get a chance to really prove himself worthy.

CHAPTER NINE

A community gymnasium sat on the edge of town, serving multiple purposes in the small community of Vernon. During the week, schools used the auditorium for their physical education exercises. There were groups who also used it for indoor sports games or lyming, parties and other social gatherings. They also had an in-built sports bar that was occasioned by men coming in from work in the evenings who tried to delay their arrival home in an attempt to relieve their stress.

On Sundays, the community church rented the facilities for a day service in the morning and a youth gathering in the evenings. It was a common facility for the community, so they usually had a full house. A lot of young people gravitated towards this church and a lot of non-Christians came in from time to time to fulfill some deep-seated religious obligation.

The guys agreed through group chat where they were going to meet so they could arrive at youth group together. Mitch had errands to run, so she wouldn't be able to make it. Devin had exited the group. Isaac was still in transit to Europe. He had texted the group during one of their layovers to let them know he was okay and that he already missed the whole bunch of them. He even mentioned that they should ensure that they prayed for Devin and not give up on him.

Christian was the first one there and prayed silently as he waited, *"Heavenly Father, I thank You for touching the heart of my friends to accept the invitation to partake at Your table tonight. Now, Spirit of Light, shine in each one of them, let them see Jesus. Open their eyes as they get the opportunity to enjoy the service and bless our pastor as he teaches on the mysteries of the trinitarian gospel. Enable him to unveil your heart like never before. In Christ I pray, Amen!"*

AJ and Dominic walked up together, and Colton and Will came from another direction. As the guys huddled, Thomas walked over with his hands in his pockets. They started towards the front doors and Christian held them open as they piled in. Tons of young adults were streaming in too, and the guys clustered as they looked around. AJ was starting to branch out and say hello to people, because he planned to attend all the time. Christian brought a group over and started introducing everyone.

"Hello! Come on in here everyone!" From the makeshift stage the worship leader was getting ready to begin the service. The guitars started up and the drummer picked a slow beat. The worship music was gorgeous and the voices on the stage sounded like they should be on the radio. The guys looked around and instead of thinking about the lone Christian believer in their group, they realized they were surrounded by people who loved Jesus. Other young adults were lost in worship, singing their hearts out, and the lights were dim enough that they could easily feel alone in their worship by closing their eyes, if that was how they preferred it.

Pastor James took the stage and began to talk to the crowd. He took a quick offering, and said, "We are going to keep the message somewhat short, as we have field day events after service and pizza. Everybody likes pizza, right? Remember field day in middle school? We're going to do a young adult version and have a blast."

The crowd gave their consent, and the guys who were there for the first time looked around again, a little shocked that the crowd was this active, large, and up for doing fun stuff. Part of their trepidation about going to church had always been that it was boring, and while it was not about the fun, it definitely helped to have an avenue for entertainment.

Pastor James paced as he talked, wearing a pinstripe suit with great shoes. Thomas noticed because this is how he would dress if he had somewhere to go, looking that sharp. "Tonight, I want to talk about ***You Are Valuable Beyond Measure.***" The message was timely and delivered with just enough Pentecostal charisma to keep it interesting. The thoughts shared were not entirely new to the visitors because Christian had been saying a lot of the same things, but it still felt like a fresh perspective.

"All over the world today, there's a distorted gospel that is being preached to the masses. It is not leaving people aware of Christ in them but aware of their wrongdoing and inability to access God directly. It's very sad, because our generation and the one to come need to know the real Jesus. The gospel of Christ is supposed to open the eyes of those who can't see, so that they may see and know that they're in Jesus and He is in them as well. People around us are looking to be accepted, loved, included. They can't find it anywhere, and honestly, some think it's even worst to go around being 'Christian folks.' I want to announce to you that - you are valuable, you are loved, and someone knows you even better than you know yourself. There is an image and likeness imprinted upon your being that is the basis of your value -- a value beyond your biggest dreams. Coins used to have the face of the person who guaranteed their value minted right there onto them. Any note or coin has a guarantor, a person or institution that guarantees its value. Even if a coin gets lost, the coin never loses its value. The one who created and designed you stamped you with His own image and likeness. He knows you better than you know yourself … He knew you even before you were born. You might not know Him, but He has always known you. You might not be aware of Him, but He has always had you on His mind. You might think … Why would anyone have such an obsession with me? Well, the Creator of this universe sees a value and a beauty in you beyond anything in this natural world. He even sees a possibility of romance!"

The crowd is responding to the beauty of the message revealed, everyone responding their own way, clapping hands, shouting, and jumping from their seats. The joy of being free through the gospel was amazing, almost like electricity in the auditorium, and it was contagious. Some of the guys were shifting in their seat, unsure how to respond to the soft caress of God's Word on their inner being.

"Whatever age you are, you have a beginning that cannot be measured in time. You have the most awesome origin. In the beginning, before creation, before time as we experience it, before the existence of evil, there was a dynamic exchange of love, a relationship without boundaries, an enjoyment of total abandonment … a being we now call God. It was in the very midst of this fiery love, at the core of this passion, that the idea of you came into being. The God who is love planned to share this love with beings created in His image and likeness. This God, who is all-knowing and able to accomplish all His purposes, planned a love affair that would span eons and conclude with a final victory in which His love conquered all – no contradiction, no evil. This good news is not some new idea, but the ancient, original thought of God. Let's imagine this beginning, let's allow the Spirit of God to draw us to this place in which all things had their origin.

Although no science can explain it, although the greatest minds have tried and failed to define it, God is confident that you are able to comprehend the unsearchable; to appreciate the motivation that birthed you; to remember where you began. In this place there is no space, yet no limit; no creation, yet no emptiness – there is only God in all His fullness. He is not lonely or in lack. It is out of His fullness, out of the overflow of love that you are conceived. God did not imagine a pet that would simply entertain Him. This God-dream is about a being who has the capacity to intelligently appreciate, to receive, to produce and to exchange the same quality of love that flows within God. His plan is not vague or speculative philosophy, but clear and specific. So clear, that He uniquely identifies and names the individuals who would form part of the plan and become part of creation. And so, before the foundation of this world, He saw you in Christ. At this point, He made up His mind about you! No matter what detours, no matter what contradictions would come, He determined that you would be His treasure – blameless and without reproach before Him in love. When did you begin? Before creation, before time itself. Where did you begin? In the very heart of love, a love relationship we call God. Why did you begin? To be loved, adored and ultimately for that love to be awakened in you."

The auditorium was jumping now. People were standing all over the place, clapping and praising God.

Pastor James flipped through the pages of his Bible and found a particular text.

"The original, authentic Word was face to face with God from the very beginning. God Himself is the content of this communication – revealing His personal presence and unique expression in all that exists. In fact, there is nothing original or innovative outside of Him. He is the only Creator and the source of all inspiration and creativity. Everything that is, has 'Made by God' stamped on its existence. The very life of God is what ignited the existence of man. This original light still shines even in darkness and no amount of darkness can put this light out."

He closed the Bible.

"The time lapse between the original thought of God and now is obviously vast. Has this original thought not been lost through time? No, this authentic dream began before time and was preserved, set apart in a person called Jesus Christ. In Him the logic of God was kept until the right time when it was made visible in flesh. He came and demonstrated in human form the kind of life God had in mind from the very beginning … a life where God and man are so united that we cannot even tell them apart. Man began in God. No matter how far man has fallen from his original place of sonship, God has never been confused about the true identity of man. Jesus Christ is the place, the event and the person in which God and man meet once again. In Christ Jesus, God has taken the initiative to reconcile man back to Himself – to restore man to a blameless state. Jesus Christ is fully God and fully man, and as such does not only represent God's initiative, He also represents man's perfect response of faith to God's initiative. Jesus reveals the heart of God more than any other story ever told or any Scripture ever written. In Him God reveals that He does not want to be God apart from us. He does not want to be a distant or unknowable God. The only way in which He wants to be God, is with man, in man, and as man. Jesus reveals the truth about man more accurately than any other story or even the factual history of man. In Him we see that the only way to be fully man, the only way to be fully free, is in union with God. This passion of God to restore man to that place of unity, would drive Him to pay any price, to go to any depth to see it accomplished. And so, in the act of becoming man, He places Himself in a position of conflict. Everything that has ever stood between God and man, every obstacle and every form of separation would meet and come to a final conclusion in this God-man, Christ Jesus. When your timeless Creator became a man, He mystically united Himself with you, so that He could bring an end to everything that stood between you and release you to be fully and truly yourself again. In this unity He faced everything you faced … and conquered. In His death, you died. That old state of being, separated from Him and united with sin, was brought to a final end in Him. He has wiped your slate clean, forgiven you of every wrongdoing. In His resurrection, you were resurrected to newness of life – that original life God imagined for you from the beginning. In His ascension, you were raised to the most glorious place of honor – a place where God delights in you. The only thing that has ever kept you from enjoying these realities, is blindness. Not seeing what He sees keeps us from enjoying what He enjoys. But these very words you are hearing now, are reminding you of your union with Him."

People were standing all over the auditorium clapping again and again. It was always difficult for Pastor James to stop people from rejoicing in the presence of the accurate gospel of Jesus. More than half of the crowd was in tears of joy and thanksgiving toward God. The message touched everyone who heard it.

"You might ask, what should I do … how does one respond to such news? Well the good news is that the hard work has already been done for you. Jesus defeated everything that stood between you. Gratitude … love awakened, is all that's left to do."

AJ was excited. What a great message of freedom and love for all of us. Christian just prayed the guys would see Jesus for who He really was. Each of the group was lost in their own thoughts, while the pastor took a drink of water and caught up with his notes, flipping through the pages.

Dominic was fighting a war within himself. *God can't forgive me. He let this stuff happen to me. That doesn't make sense, if He loves me. How can He love me? Free? Does that mean the memories too? And how could He forgive my uncle? How could He set him free when He did this stuff? I wish I could ask all these things, but I can't...*

Thomas wanted to be a part of this Jesus movement. *I want to know how to be a part of this relationship. Freedom and love...life isn't good or bad, it's boring. There is a purpose to Jesus, and I can bring this freedom to others? I hope they tell us how to start a relationship.*

Will was struggling. *This stuff is cool. It's not on TV and I enjoyed it anyhow? Why isn't there a show about this guy? He's cooler than a superhero, choosing to die. How can He feel after doing all that when we choose to do whatever we want to do?*

Colton was stuck in the past. *How could that poker night have changed? If I was with Jesus then, would He have stopped that robbery? Or would He have still let it happen? I feel like I wouldn't have even been there, but what's wrong with who I am and what I like? What about when we were homeless? Where was Jesus then? We were cold and hungry...and nobody, not even church people helped us. Nobody, man. If Jesus is real, I need to see more.*

Pastor James cleared his throat, pulling each of them away from their thoughts. "Look, any fear-based relationship has to be sustained by fear and removes all possibility for romance. God is not mad at you; He is mad about you. The simplicity of this statement puts religion out of business. Now, I want to see people breaking shackles tonight—you are shackled by fear, sometimes anger, hurt, pain. Maybe you think some incidents in your life are Jesus' fault, or you're wondering where He was in that moment."

"Is he reading my thoughts, " Colton was confused.

"I am going to tell you, friends, don't allow philosophy to tease you into embracing your uncertainties when there is a gospel that wants to persuade you of God's unwavering care and love for you. Jesus isn't the cause of anything bad. The Bible says that everything good comes from God. Every perfect gift is from Him. These good gifts come down from the Father who made all the lights in the sky. But God never changes like the shadows from those lights. He is always the same. I will let you go with these thoughts. Turn your focus inward, rather than outward. Become aware of the One who made you and united Himself with you. He is within you. Even at your weakest, He remains your full strength. For with Him, nothing is impossible. In your own thoughts and words, respond to His love. You can say something as simple as: 'Thank you, Lord, for who You are and what You have done for me. As You gave yourself in love to me, I give myself in love to You. You made me in Your image and likeness, I acknowledge Your ownership. You made me to be loved so here I am, love me.'"

Young people were crying all over the auditorium. Love filled the room, no one was distracted, everyone was deep in their thoughts.

"Some people tonight are being healed of things inside that they might not even speak out loud to anyone in the world. He still knows, and His heart breaks with you. Whatever you have known about God that is unlike Jesus Christ, is not God. If you have seen Jesus, you have seen the Father. This was His purpose, to resonate and redeem the Abba echo in every human's heart. I am going to ask that anyone who is saying in their own heart right now: 'Here I am Jesus, love me. I give myself in love to You, just as You gave Yourself in love to me.' If you are that person, come on up here. Don't stand in your place or sit there and end up crying or complaining. I can't make you step out, but I am going to start a countdown. Ten: don't worry about the people around you, if you want to make the decision to live your relationship with Jesus, come on down and let's pray together. Nine: this isn't about your pride or your ego, this is about a love story between you and Papa God—would you make it up here to see His salvific life igniting within the heart, mind and soul of one of your parents or siblings? Why not for yourself? Eight: I see you coming, this will be a day you remember for the rest of your life. Seven: freedom, peace, happiness are at the table for you to partake of, right here and right now. Six: …"

Thomas wasn't listening to the countdown anymore; he was making his way to the front. His heart was pleading with his brain to be smart, and his brain was begging for this to be real. He wasn't sure what would be left if it wasn't real. He had watched Christian and AJ go through something crazy and turn to a lot of different people. He had seen how much they had changed and admitted they were complete in Jesus and with Jesus. He wanted what he saw in his friends.

Colton and Will weren't ready, not yet. They kept their heads down and were respectful of the process, but they were looking forward to what was coming after the service; free drinks, pizza and gladiator-style games, sounded like fun. They were both grappling with the desire to come back, but it was uncomfortable sitting when most of the people in the auditorium were making their way to the front. They enjoyed the message given by Pastor James, but for them it all sounded too good to be true. They didn't feel ready to go with the other youths, at least not yet.

Dominic was really struggling. He wanted to see, but anger boiled up and stopped him from going up just yet. He had a request, but it could wait.

Isaac was sitting with his parents in the airport waiting for a connecting flight. He was reading a recent article published about two rival gangs at war in their community. Of great concern was the fact that he knew Devin was involved with one of the gangs. He shared the article in the group chat.

Thousands of miles away, Mitch was the first to see the article posted, but she was not surprised. She doesn't make a habit of reading the daily news because it was all bad, but she was also aware of what was happening because she knew her brother was involved. She stopped packing out groceries to read the full article. She was unaware that two rivalling gang members armed with handguns just sneaked through a window upstairs.

CHAPTER TEN

Dominic sat on the pavement outside the gym watching as people mulled about waiting for the evening to begin. His thoughts had turned to mush while he tried to process the revelations of the evening. There seemed to be a conflict within his being as if the new ideas presented had met on an opposing force that refused to allow the thoughts to take root and germinate. It was the war between ideologies and truth. He knew everyone had their own idea of what was truth based on their own experience and background growing up. Personality, character, and beliefs are formed by life's experiences and may even feel as if they were cemented. Dominic was conflicted; he was not sure what to do with himself. He got up to join the others.

The church staff started directing the young adults toward the cafeteria where there were different stations. The staff gave each participating young adult a colored wristband and a card to fill out their event information on, so they could determine a winning team at the end.

The guys all checked out their wristbands. Christian had white, Will had red, Colton blue, and Dominic received yellow. AJ had green, and Thomas had orange. Pastor James had changed into workout pants and a T-shirt.

"Let's get the games started! Quiet down while we tell you the rules. We have stations, and you're going to huddle with your team. Each person is going to do three events…each team will make sure each event is covered. You'll pick the top times in each event to put forward for team stats. That means you win and lose as a team. Get together by color!"

Everyone started looking at each other's wrists, until someone took charge and called out, "Red over here…" Everyone found where they needed to go. There were several color groups to help everyone get to an event, and the huddle forced everyone to talk as they planned for each person to compete in their best events. There were several events: the potato sack race, egg run, water run, races in a few lengths, free shot throw, ring toss, and tons of others.

After the teams were in clusters, people started going toward their events. There were three lines on each paper that allowed the competitors to write their results. Will decided to go on the throwing games, and he did pretty well. There was another bigger guy who decided to stick with him during the huddle and do the same events. His name was Blake, and he wanted to chat. "How long have you been coming here?"

Will was smiling without even realizing. "This is my first time."

"Oh man, that's awesome, I'm glad you came. What did ya think?" Blake lit up hearing this, excited to meet someone on their first visit. His own first time had been a blast and the people he met then remained his friends to this day. Blake meant to welcome Will so he might open up to receive the word of Christ.

"It was okay. That Jesus character seems unreal, like too good to be true, and you know what they say; if it's too good to be true, it probably is." Will spoke freely because he had been so moved by the whole situation, he couldn't even fake a different answer. Besides, he wanted to hear what Blake had to say about it.

"Dude, He is real. When I started coming here, I had cancer. I was seriously sick; I can't even start telling you how bad it was. I was pretty out of it, not really understanding how in my early twenties I was already facing the 'c' word. I was torn up. I kept hearing about the stripes Jesus took for my healing, His love for me, grace, me being in Christ and Christ being in me and I thought the same thing—He might heal, but He won't heal me…right?"

Blake's face remained happy, even talking about such a terrible disease at such a young age and it hit home with Will, who had lost several family members to cancer and he knew the suffering, the pain, the desperation they endured before dying. He looked at Blake with compassion and imagined him going through the same things. "I'm sorry about your cancer, you seem like a good guy." Will felt horrible that Blake had to deal with this. It put a stark perspective on their youth.

"Dude! Hold on! I don't have cancer anymore!" Blake chuckled, holding his hands up.

"You said you had cancer…had…gotcha, so you had surgery or did you do chemo?" Will felt silly for jumping to an apology, but he pressed on. Blake seemed nice, and he thought he would like to know more about his new friend.

"It's cool! I kept hearing people talking about it, about healing that has been made available for us in Christ, and one day I left church and got to my dorm room. And I was tormented by thoughts that I would die and my whole life was worthless."

He was trying not to be too emotional about it, but Will found Blake's story really affecting. He wanted to be a tough guy, but he could feel the ache of tears behind his eyes. He had lost older family members to cancer and seeing someone so young going through it was overwhelming.

Blake saw that Will was choked up and hurried on. "I hit my knees and said, 'Dear God, if You're real, if You gave Jesus to come and redeem Your image and likeness in me, please heal me today. Give me a chance to love

You with all I am and be loved by You, and I will make Your love known to my friends and family, even Your kindness, mercy and healing power. Because Jesus died for me, thank You for giving me life, and life abundantly, in Jesus' name.' I didn't feel any different right at that moment. I struggled with thoughts telling me I hadn't been healed, that I would just die, and that God didn't care about me, that I wasn't pure enough for God to listen to me and do something about the situation I was in. I fought through them and kept studying the Word of God, beholding the face of Jesus and I discovered that healing was already provided in me through the redemptive work of Christ Jesus. I believed and started to see myself free in God, I agreed with what He said about me. Then, there was a day I came to church gathering and the wife of the pastor was talking about 'How to deconstruct and unlearn something concerning you that you are struggling with.' She said: You don't have to extract the drought first. We should let the water deal with it and watch the space transform naturally. Her point was this: Light dispels darkness effortlessly. Since that day, I stopped struggling in my own mind and my heart. I started to testify to anyone who would hear me that I was healed in Jesus' name. Without even knowing yet what the result was, I had received it in my spirit, in my mind, in my thoughts, I kept meditating and seeing myself growing, having a family and completely free from cancer. When I went to the doctor a month later for my next bad-news session, they couldn't find a trace of cancer in my body. Just as if I was never diagnosed cancer positive before. I have been cancer-free for almost a year now. I couldn't help myself, I cried for a whole week, and up to today when I worship God, I simply see my life as a miracle and living testimony. There is no going back for me." Blake gave Will a huge smile and put his hands together in praying-mode.

Will had no words to answer Blake. He just blinked at him, his mouth slightly open. Jesus seemed amazing, but he still couldn't figure out why Jesus would love him. But the thought of being healed from cancer would chisel large chunks out of the wall of doubt that God was real.

"Man, I am glad that you're okay now. Did you tell the doctors that prayers healed you? You had cancer though. That must have been really deep."

"It was. But we're here to have fun, so let's lighten this up." Blake started asking the normal questions like what his favorite TV show was, and school stuff. Will was comfortable on this terrain and started to relax, realizing he was thoroughly enjoying himself.

Thomas had gone to the front after the service, and he was still working through the new feelings inside. He wanted to talk to Christian about the changes he was feeling. As his group was planning their events, Thomas' mind was elsewhere until a girl with a really pretty smile spoke to him. "Hi. I'm Jenna." The other people on the orange team started off in a different direction. "Do you want to walk with me?"

"That would be good, thanks." Thomas fell in step with her as they walked toward the three-legged race.

"I'll watch, I don't want to do this one." Thomas wasn't focused enough on the games to excel at this event.

"Silly, I need a partner. Anyway, you agreed." Her smile was really blinding, and Thomas found himself smiling back unable to refuse her. As they got ready to race, he couldn't stop imagining falling flat on his face and taking Jenna with him.

"If I'm no good at this, remember that I warned you ahead of time and you insisted." He was pleasantly surprised by her cute laugh, and that he made it happen.

"Deal. Just say 'step' and that will be when we step together."

"Deal."

The event leader called, "READY? Set. GO!" Jenna and Thomas took off, sticking to the method they agreed on. When they finished first, Jenna gave him a huge high-five and he realized he was having a blast.

"I need a drink, I'm so thirsty," she said after the leader put their time on their card. They started walking towards the refreshment tables. "Are you having fun?"

"Yeah, I really am."

"You seem lost in thought. Want to talk about it?" Jenna seemed genuine, and Thomas shrugged.

"I went to the front tonight, and I said to Jesus: Just as He gave himself in love for me, here I am, I give myself to Him in love as well, no holding anything back. There is a lot I need to know. I already feel different, and I keep trying to understand the fullness of what I am feeling. How can I even explain this to anyone? I've never felt anything like this in my whole life! What now?" Thomas hoped she had an answer or at least she might take him to someone who does.

"That's great! You know this is just the beginning, right?!" Jenna must be a cheerleader in another life, because she does a mini-two clap jump and squeal. It made Thomas' eyebrows shot up.

"What's next, though? I really don't know." The uncertainty in Thomas' voice was clear, and Jenna curbed her enthusiasm long enough to take him to a team leader, where she encouraged him to talk. Thomas agreed and told Greg about his decision. Greg told Jenna to go back to the games, and he spent time answering as many questions as Thomas could think to ask.

Colton was looking forward to the competition. He was a natural born sportsman who was often compared to famous athletes who crossed from football to basketball to baseball in the pros. The question wasn't whether he would go pro but what sport he would go pro in. He was serious about the events he chose, and his adrenaline surged while he was getting himself ready. Winning was always the only option for him.

There was another guy who was an athlete too. His name was Mike and he was a little older. He stood in front of his companions and noticed that Colton was treating the field day events like they were the Olympic preliminaries. Mike decided to compete where he was the best and challenged Colton to show him that he could have fun tonight too. They went for the foot race, and Mike told the leader who was timing the event that it was just the two of them running this time. He looked at Colton and sent him a defiant look. "You ready, kid?"

"Aww man, you gonna lose."

Mike readied up. "We'll see,"

"Ready. Set. GO!" The two guys took off. Once they reached the wall they headed back, and Mike pulled ahead. Colton pushed himself as hard as he could but still came in behind Mike.

"Man!" Colton was winded and astonished. "Where'd you learn to run like that?"

Mike laughed. "I've been running all my life, and I ran in college."

"You're fast, dude! I could barely keep up! You gotta tell me your secret!" Colton wanted to build a friendship with this guy. He could see them training together. Mike could make him a better athlete, and sports was his way out of this town.

"It's a deal - if you take your time and have fun tonight. What did you think about service tonight, by the way? I don't think I've seen you here before, and I would remember."

"The service was cool. I need to hear more before I'm in. It's compelling though, really interesting stuff." Colton knew this guy was probably all in with the Jesus stuff, if he went to this church on the regular, but he was always going to be honest and real. It didn't matter to him if people found him gruff. He would rather be known for who he truly was. Who wanted to put on a front everywhere they went? That was far too much work.

"I understand that, and I challenge you to come a few more times. There are good people here, and you might learn something as well." Colton reminded Mike of who he was five years ago, so he knew how to speak to him to get him to stick around. The good news of Christ was the rescuing act of God that saved everyone equally. It was not understood right away, and Mike wanted to leave an open door, and an invitation for Colton to know more about Jesus, His Father and Holy Spirit. Colton was obviously the type who had to come to his own conclusions. "Let's do the potato sack race. That one takes real skill. Let's see if you've got any." Colton grinned, and the two started out to join the next event.

Dominic had been lost in himself for a while. The weight of his past was becoming overwhelming. As soon as the yellow team broke, Dominic went looking for Pastor James. He had kept his eyes on him ever since the colors were collecting themselves into teams.

"Pastor, can I talk to you alone?" Dominic didn't mean to seem so desperate, but it was obvious he was pleading. Pastor James looked him over and nodded with a smile.

"Sure, let's head back to the auditorium. We'll have some privacy there." The guys walked in silence until they were alone. "What's your name?"

"Dominic." That's all he could muster as he tried to find the courage to say what he wanted to say, what he needed to share so he could get guidance. Christian had told him that this was an option. If he wanted out, he needed to make that decision before he spoke. Once he started speaking, there was no turning back. He had noticed that things Christian had brought up in the past had come up in tonight's sermon, and that was a sign to Dominic that this might be the time to speak to an adult.

A few miles from the church, the house where Devin lived was being cordoned off with caution tape by two uniformed Policemen. An ambulance was present with lights blazing, and sirens could be heard approaching the location in the distant. Neighbors were gathering, but kept in check by police personnel behind the tape as they tried to ascertain what had transpired in their neighborhood.

A black jaguar pulls up on the curb just outside the cordoned off area. Devin jumped from the car. The Boss is sitting behind the driver's wheel. He lights a cigarette as he watched Devin try to get through the security line.

"I live here!" Devin protested, and he was allowed to pass. He ducked below the tape and ran towards the house. Grace was being escorted out, weeping uncontrollably. Devin could feel his inside growing solid with trepidation.

"Mom, what's going on?"

Grace wanted to speak, but the words wouldn't come. She knew it was Devin's fault and she wanted him to know there and then, but her throat was blocked from overwhelming emotions.

"Mom, you need to talk to me. Tell me what's going --"

Grace pointed towards the front door.

"You did this!"

A gurney was pushed through the front door with a bloody white sheet covering a body. Devin's heart sank into his stomach as he stopped the medics from going any further, until he saw who was under that sheet. Devin pulled the sheet back and broke when he saw his lifeless sister lying on the gurney. Her eyes were still open from the fright of the last image she saw, but she was cold. Devin knew he had brought trouble home. He knew Grace would blame it on him. He knew his sister was dead because of him.

Devin staggered back towards the car. Some of his neighbors tried to get him to tell them what was happening, but the world had gone silent. Devin heard nothing but the beating of his heart and the thoughts of vengeance and anger. He got in the car, and no words needed to be spoken between him and the Boss. An all-out gang war was imminent. Someone was gonna pay big time.

§

"It's good to meet you, Dominic. Let's move past this nice stuff and talk. Something is obviously bothering you."

"Ummm, there's this situation. I know I have to tell you about it, but I don't think I can do this…" Dominic felt like he couldn't think clearly because this could cause so much trouble for his family. He lowered his head and stared at the floor. The need to get it out of his system was so strong, but there was something jamming his throat.

"Son, you're safe to talk about whatever you need to with me. I'm not going to judge you, but I will do whatever I can to help." Pastor James paused to give Dominic a chance to talk, and when he noticed Dominic's tough guy exterior was cracking, he pushed gently. "Maybe it's none of my business, but you seem to want to get this weight, whatever it is, off your shoulders. Nothing can shock me. The guy I serve was nailed to a cross by His hands and feet, and He gave up His own life for whatever it is you think is so horrible."

Dominic looked up. "How did He give His life? They nailed him to a cross. Not trying to be rude, but Jesus didn't really have a choice." He tried to smile to soften his words, but he still didn't know what to make of the Jesus stuff being preached.

"Is that what you think? That's an interesting take on it, bud." Pastor James' voice was calm, not confrontational. Dominic was in a challenging mood though. He wanted an excuse to run far away from that place and everything burning on the inside of him.

"That's what it is…the blood, right? Y'all say He rose, but where's the proof?" Dominic was crumbling, he was almost making their point for them and he choked a little.

Pastor smiled but steered the conversation back to Dominic's issues. "Everywhere. Look, you're hurting. We can talk about whether He is real, whether He rose, but I think you already know the answers. What is really going on?" Pastor James had more compassion than anyone Dominic had ever met, and he decided he never had to come back if this didn't go well.

"I'm so ashamed, but I need advice. My uncle…he did stuff to me when I was little. I have a little brother, he did stuff to him too. All I can think about is killing him, but I know that's not the right thing to do. He's family."

"I'm following you." Pastor James was deep in thought and prayer, but he didn't seem to be up in arms over what he was hearing.

Dominic continued. "I hated God for a while, like - why me? I didn't want that! I'm worried my 'sicko' uncle will hurt other little boys and someone needs to stop him. That stuff he did to me when I couldn't defend myself has ruined my life. I've done all kinds of stuff to try and stop it hurting." Dominic paused, and looked at Pastor James expression, trying to find something that would provoke him to stop talking. There was nothing but compassion, an irresistible invitation just to pour it all out. "I've been with guys and girls, I watched inappropriate videos, and none of that is doing anything for me. I'm miserable, and it's my uncle's fault. If he could do that to me, think what he must have done to my little brother! I'm very tired of running to the wrong places to make it better. Ain't nobody safe or worth anything to my life since that happened…"

Dominic looked at Pastor James, who simply nodded in understanding, staying quiet so Dominic could get it all out.

"It's lonely, man. Me and my friends talked a lot about the emptiness inside but can't find a way out. There's no light shining at the end of no tunnel for us. We're all going through the same, ya´know. Our dude Christian became a believer here and probably had the most difficult life of us all, losing his parents and grandparents, being an orphan, institutionalized…but he sure seems happy now. He told us about love filling the void. He is always talking to us about the love of God, Jesus, peace, kindness. He kept reminding us that as long as we won't rest on the love of God, we will always feel like we are missing something. I feel like there's nothing there anymore. How can anyone fill this emptiness, when the hole is gaping and dangerous? I hate people, I have trust issues, and I'm getting to the point that I don't care at all, not whether I hurt anyone. There is no way your innocent Jesus can accept me, not after everything I've done." Dominic's head dropped; his tone hopeless.

Pastor James sensed Dominic was done talking. He waited a few more seconds just to make sure before speaking. "Okay, I'm going to get to everything you just said. We are going to talk about you first, because you are important, and then we'll talk about the situation with your uncle afterwards. Does that work for you?"

"Yes, sir. I guess."

"I can't approach this without the Word of Christ. Can you give me that Bible next to you?"

"Yes." Dominic grabbed a small Bible that was on the seat next to him and gave it to Pastor James.

"Cool, thanks. So here we go." Pastor James pulled out his reading glasses from the bag he had strapped over his shoulder. He appeared to have been equipped and ready for this moment. "First of all, it's written in Psalms 147:3 that God heals the brokenhearted, His Spirit will heal the sorrows of your heart and bind up the wounds. I want you to understand that Jesus doesn't need to receive you today, He received you already. Before you were born, He already knew you, had chosen you and placed you in His family. You are not the product of your mother's womb; you began in God. You should live your life from the completeness that God's Sabbath celebrates. He rests in his love and dances over you with joy according to the Scriptures. God says, 'But if we confess our sins, God will forgive us.' This mean that when we communicate what God says about our sins, we discover what He believes concerning our redeemed identity. We are cleansed from every distortion we believe about ourselves. Therefore, to claim innocence by our own efforts under the law of personal performance is to deceive ourselves, and to deliberately ignore the truth. The truth is that you are holy, blameless and righteous in the eyes of God - but this doesn't mean you have to go into denial if you have done something wrong."

Dominic paid close attention to what Pastor James was saying.

"Brother, all you have to do is talk with God. He is a good Father who cares about every single detail of your life. When I look at you, I can tell you are tired of living with the memories of what happened, and everything that happened because of how you felt at that moment. Jesus loves you just as you are right now. I believe each time you talk to Jesus, you will not be the same - you will be changed in your mind and heart. What really needs changing is what you believe about who God is to you, and what you believe about yourself."

"What if I mess up? What if I do something really terrible?" asked Dominic, his voice choking a little.

"Don't get me wrong, I'm not telling you that you won't do anything wrong anymore - but what I am sure of is that the good work God begins in you will continue until He completes it. Learn to love yourself in the light of God's opinion of you. Here is an amazing thought to always have in your heart: 'When anyone is in Christ, it is a whole new world. The old things are gone; suddenly, everything is new!' Paul is telling us that now in the light of our co-inclusion in His death and resurrection, whoever you thought you were before, in Christ you are a brand-new person. The old ways of seeing yourself and everyone else are over. Acquaint yourself with the new."

"This sounds pretty cool, pastor. You wanna say I will change even physically?"

Pastor James laughed. "No, Dominic, of course not – look, you made me laugh. You don't get a new body or just suddenly forget the past."

"Oh, that's okay then, but it would be cool if I could get a new look, right?" Dominic's smiling a little, some of the tension relieved now that he had managed to get the words out and hadn't got in trouble for them.

Pastor James was trying to make it easy for Dominic to understand. "Just picture a Jew, Greek, slave, free, black, white, African, American, European, Asian, Muslim, Protestant, imagine all these categories of people, all of them dead and gone for good. They all died when Jesus died, no one is left in the entire planet. So, the life you have been given to live when He rose from the dead is a brand-new life. You start enjoying the beauty of this life when you stop trying to control and design whatever you want or think, and now you can start discovering who you have always been in God's eyes, and all that has been given to you freely by joyfully engaging your thoughts with resurrection realities. You are in Christ by God's doing, not yours. You are redeemed, co-raised and co-seated together with Christ."

"I feel like I'm in a bit of a dream right now. Can I record some of the things you're telling me?"

Pastor James looked happy that Dominic was trying to grasp what he was hearing, and that he wanted to make sure he could revisit the conversation later. "Absolutely, this is freedom indeed! Was I making sense?"

Dominic found the sound recorder app on his cell phone and pressed record.

"Sorta, I think so. In this relationship, anytime I do something wrong and ask for forgiveness, I am forgiven. I also understood that I am a brand-new person, that the old stuff is gone, everything became new because I died when Jesus died. It doesn't matter who I am and where I am from, I got that. It sounds great, just not realistic enough." Dominic was trying to understand the concept, but it was not as clear as he would like. Life had taught him that some people were valued more than others, and Pastor James was sitting there, challenging all the things that were familiar. He agreed more with what he was hearing, but that wasn't the point. It didn't match up to Dominic's experiences, and those were more real to him.

Although the puzzle was not complete in his head, Dominic thought he had learnt the main lesson, and he would find the new pieces as he walked the new horizon that had been opened for him. The more he heard the gospel of Christ, the more it changed his entire world.

"I understand that. I don't want to tie up all your time while everyone hangs out, but we can take as much time as you need or want. As for the situation at home, have you talked to your parents about your uncle."

"It's just my mom." Dominic said, "She didn't believe me when it first happened because she needed him around. But when my little brother told her the same story, she broke. We hardly speak these days because I think she is so ashamed and really doesn't know how to relate to us."

"You are a good kid, and fear can immobilize a person. I guess your mom knows, and I'm guessing, this uncle is related to her?"

"Yeah. Her brother."

"Okay - and you did well to talk about how you feel about this whole thing. Try talking to her. If you don't want to do it alone, I can come with you for moral support. She needs help too." Pastor James was sincere in everything he said, that much was apparent even to Dominic. They continued to talk, and Dominic challenged

186

some things. This was nothing new or daunting to Pastor James. He was ready with Scriptures, in a loving way, at every turn in the conversation.

The day was winding down back at the games. The guys ended up at the one event at the same time, and Colton directly challenged Christian. Christian hadn't done his three events yet, and Colton had just one more. Everyone knew Colton was an athlete, someone who was no stranger to lifting weights at the gym and playing contact sports. But although Colton was very serious about his athletic life, he was laughing to be up against his lifelong friend.

The team leaders put elbow and knee pads on the guys, then helmets with face masks. Colton had his game face on under the mask, and Christian stepped up onto the balancing pad the two of them must stand on while holding huge padded battle sticks.

"Get ready! Get Set! SPAR!" the leader called. By this time, a lot of the young adults were watching, because it was the most interesting of the field day events.

Colton and Christian jab at each other for a few moments as they got their bearings. Christian was laughing at every move, having a great time. He had never done anything like this before, and he was grateful to the church for the experience. It was a little different for Colton. He got stuck in his own head. He had so much anger stored up. With every new hit, he got more aggressive and his mind released torrents of the hurt that had been buried for too long.

HIT. *Mom left me, she just left with no warning. There was nothing I could do or say to change it. She died, and I will never see her again.*

HIT. *Your parents died too, and you just get over it by replacing them with Jesus. Your new relationship doesn't fix your life, man.*

HIT. *All I have is fake friends, outside of you. God, it makes me so angry.*

HIT. *Gotta live up to my dad's standard and expectations.*

HIT. *My only chance is to go pro. If I don't do that, I will be stuck in a life I have no interest in. I don't even know where to start outside of sports.*

Colton was raining down hits on Christian in quick succession. Christian flew off the pad and Colton jumped down to continue hitting him. Christian had never done anything to Colton except try to be a friend, but he curled up to take the punches. His refusal to fight back sent Colton into frenzied tears. "Hit me back, man…c'mon. Aren't you sick of life breaking you? FIGHT BACK."

The team leader fetched help to stop Colton and Pastor James said, "Come over here and sit with me, Colton." Colton had tears streaming down his face. He didn't quite know what happened or felt he had the power to stop himself. It had started out in good fun.

"What happened out there? Aren't you two friends?" Pastor James spoke softly and easy, inviting Colton to respond instead of ordering him.

"Yes. He's probably my only real friend. I don't really know what happened. It's like I just started hitting him and all these thoughts about what's wrong in my life were powering my hands. Every hit was a new sentence I needed to get out of my system and all of a sudden, he was my enemy, and I just wanted him to fight back in life. He's different since he started coming here."

Pastor James nodded. "Any awakening journey we embark on should not distant us from our friends, rather it should reveal love and bring us closer to the "yet-to-be awakened" people around us. The great awakening befriends love; it does not deflect. Your friends simply understands the gospel. You want to hear some ancient wisdom? I'll have you tell me what you think it means, deal?"

"Sure…"

"It goes like this, 'Greater love hath no man than this, that a man lay down his life for his friends.' What does that mean to you?"

Colton thought it over and tried to answer. "If a man truly loves someone, they'll give their life for the person they love."

"That's good. What do you think about that?" Pastor James wanted to understand Colton, and the best way to do that was ask questions.

"I don't think anyone would give their life for me. That's what hurts." Colton felt fresh tears threatening to fall.

"Someone already did."

"If you are talking about Christian, he took a few punches and he's too weak to throw any. That's not laying down his life." Colton crossed his arms in front of him. He didn't want to hear Christian being put on a pedestal right now. Why couldn't it be about him for once?

"I wasn't talking about Christian, son. I'm telling you that someone loved you enough to die for you and as you. He already did, so that he could help you through exactly what you're going through." That stopped Colton, but he couldn't help sounding defensive.

"Oh, more Jesus stuff. How do you know? I am not trying to be rude, man, but how do you know for sure that it's real? What if it's not, and you've lived your whole life being good and chasing nothing? Your whole life would have been wasted on this junk."

"What if you're right? If it was all for nothing, I have been kind and loving to every person that I could. I have lived conscious of Jesus' presence in me and with me in everything that I do—giving to the orphans and widows, feeding the hungry, clothing the naked. Isn't that better than just trying to be a famous person who does nothing but perform for those watching them?"

"True, true."

"What if you're wrong though? What if it is just as I teach, that God created the heavens and the earth and that Jesus died for and as your sins, and mine, and every other person simply to redeem us from our darkness and its influences, loss, pain, disappointment, death? You have been reconnected to God your Father through the death and resurrection of Jesus Christ." Pastor James paused to let this sink in.

"Then I'd be in trouble. I have a long life ahead of me though, I have time." Colton wasn't ready to make the changes he had seen Christian make in his life. "We are young. Why do we have to make this decision now?"

"Jesus did not come to convince you to make a choice or to politely apologize on his Father's behalf for a faulty design. He came to prove that God did not make a mistake when He made you. He rescued you from the lies that you probably still believe about yourself. That lie died. The original authentic you revived and is right here in front of me. If you could just journey with God and see how amazing you are, you might be tempted to worship yourself thinking you are God. Remember, Jesus who knew no sin embraced our distortion, our blindness, shame, failure, pain, rejection, weaknesses, fears, doubts, etc. He appeared to be without form, this was the mystery of God's prophetic poetry. He was disguised in our distorted image, marred with our iniquities, He took our sorrows, our pain, our shame to His grave and birthed His righteousness in us. He took our sins and we became his righteousness. The Lord has borne His holy arm before the eyes of all nations, and all the ends of the earth shall see the salvation of our God. Kings will shut their mouths because of Him; for what had not been told them, they will see, and what they had not heard, they will understand. Surely, He has borne our griefs, carried our sorrows, yet we esteemed him stricken, smitten and afflicted of God. But, he was wounded for our transgressions, he was bruised for our iniquities; the chastisement of our peace was on Him; and with His stripes, we ourselves are healed. He was not bruised by God but by the very humanity He was about to redeem. Everything I just said is a display of the love of God for the entire humanity. Can I explain to you real quick what happened to man?"

"Yeah, I'm listening."

"Alright, man [male and female] corrupted himself. He didn't behave as being part of God's family. He became a distorted being, twisted out of his true pattern, crooked and pervert. He became unmindful of the rock that begot him and forgot the God and Father who danced with him, in eternity."

"This sounds scary pastor," Colton's eyes became bigger as pastor was talking about the condition of man.

"Wait son, that is not the good news. It was simply to show you how great and loving of a Savior God in Christ is. Here is the good news; God pre-designed and engineered man from the beginning to be jointly fashioned in the same mold and image of his son according to the exact blueprint of His thought. We see the original and intended pattern of our lives preserved in His Son. Jesus Christ is the firstborn from the same womb that reveals our root." Pastor James paused to allow Colton to absorb what he was talking about. Colton enjoyed the moment and can't stop recording everything Pastor James was sharing with him. He was totally amazed and didn't even think about the clock.

"So, God was in Christ, making peace between the world and Himself. In Christ, God did not hold people guilty for their sins. He gave me this message of peace to tell people. So, I am sent to speak for Christ. I speak for Christ when I beg you to be at peace with God. Jesus confirms that we are the invention of God. We were born anew when He was raised from the dead. His resurrection reveals that we share the same origin with Him; we are of the same value and worth. No wonder He isn't ashamed to call us His brethren. You see, son, I just painted for you a picture of the grace of God. You are included in this picture, because when the Scriptures say 'Man,' it truly means all men and women. There is hope for all of us, far beyond what our human minds can comprehend. So, Bud, why waste another second believing the 'ugly duckling' lie? You're a beautiful swan by design. Look deeply into the mirror of your eyes. You're God's dream come true." Pastor James was ready to explain more but one of the staff members popped their head in and signaled for his attention. "One second, Colton."

"Pastor, we have calculated the winners, and we wanted you to make the announcement."

Pastor James said, "Can you give me a second? Keep everybody happy and excited, I'll be there in a moment." He turned to Colton, a warm smile on his face. "Can we finish this another time?"

"That's fine. But I wanted to ask you something." Colton looked a little bit disappointed. It was nice that Pastor James was taking time to speak with him.

"Sure."

"How do I reach this kind of faith? What should I do to get it and how long will that take me to be like Christian or the rest of the people I see here? I heard a lot of preachers speaking about how to get faith." Colton was trying to experience whatever his friend and all the other believers were enjoying within.

"It is kind of weird how some of my brothers and sisters out there say things like 'have faith.' It is just like instructing someone to fall in love. Faith is not something you do in order to get anything or go anywhere; it is something that happens to you upon persuasion. One doesn't choose to fall in love, they simply do, that's where the magic is. You see what is already true about you or yours. We are lovingly entangled with Father, Son and Spirit!"

"Thank you so much for your time, pastor, I really appreciate it." Colton stopped recording the conversation and kept everything in his little bag. He would spend some time to listen to everything Pastor James told him again and again to understand better what he said.

"You're welcome to stay while the team cleans up and the driver takes a handful of people home. We received word that there was another shooting in the community, something gang-related, so we need to make sure you arrive home safely." Pastor James was happy he took some time to talk to Colton. He enjoyed Colton's honesty and freedom.

"Come on then, let's go find out which team won. Which team were you on?" Colton held up his wrist to show his blue band.

"Everybody, get with your teams. We have a winner!" Pastor James waited, while everyone got into the correct teams. "I am going to countdown the top three. The second runner up is, drum roll please; WHITE TEAM, you're in third, what a fierce competition. You were only one event and thirty-two seconds off the first runner up, drum roll please; RED TEAM, you are in second."

The cheers were resounding, and the excitement mounted inside the gym. The teams not yet called grew quiet as they waited to hear who the best-of-the-best was. "Everybody, the winning team has flown under the radar all night. They won by three of the best times of the night. We are happy to give a $50 gift card to everyone on the; ORANGE TEAM!" The crowd started cheering and the orange team came up to the prize table.

The guys started drifting together and everyone talked quietly as they waited for Colton. When he saw them, he walked over. "I'll catch you guys later."

Christian sank into quiet despair as he watched him walk away. They had been friends for most of his life, and the cold dismissal after what happened between them left Christian wondering what was next.

"Hey Christian, can you come here for a second?" The pastor's wife had been looking at him.

"Yes, madam."

"I know you are a little shocked regarding what happened with Colton and that's okay. I totally understand what you feel. You are very special and unique. Here is the word of grace for your heart and mind. There is absolutely no attraction in controversy, only in love. Remain yourself and don't allow strange voices to invade your thoughts regarding your relationship with your friend. If our message is not about love and in love, then this grace we talk about becomes yet another empty philosophy. If inclusion excludes the one who disagrees with us, hurt us, reject us, abuse us or whatever wrongdoing anyone can do against us, then the whole concept is void, better just keep our mouths shut. Love believes even in the one who don't believe in love." Very lovely and sweet, the wife of the pastor couldn't see anyone feeling low or down and let them walk away without allowing the Spirit of God to minister to them through her.

"Thank you so much, madam. Can you please pray for me?"

"Sure, dear, I can do that. Let's pray. *Lord Jesus Christ, beloved, eternal and faithful Son of the Father incarnate, thank You for Your gentle mercy on Christian in his darkness. I ask You to grant to him that which he lacks in his self–faith, hope and love. Bind all forms of darkness and evil that influences his mind and heart, right now. Share with him Your own knowledge of the Father's heart, that he may know Your confidence, Your passion, Your joy and peace. Continuously reveal Your Son in him, so that he may be of service to You in Your liberation of his friends and of the human race as well. Thank You, Father, in Christ I prayed. Amen.*"

"Amen. Thank you so much. I am blessed and favored to have Pastor James and you as my leaders." Christian was sincerely grateful to have this amazing couple in his life.

Pastor offered to take the guys home, but they insisted that they would be okay. They heard rumors about a shooting but that was not uncommon. This was their neighborhood, and they grew up here. Unless you get mixed up in a gang, you are usually generally safe on the streets at any hours of the night. As the guys headed out together, a few of them bantered about the night. They came to Will's house first. Before he went in, he turned to Christian. "Forget Colton, man, that was wrong tonight. I didn't realize he was such a jerk."

"No, He is not a jerk. He might just be going through something. He is still my friend, just like you and he is forgiven." Christian was stung but he was not going to turn his back on his friend.

"Dude, you need to wake up. It's cool that you changed your life, but people like Devin and Colton can't take it and they hate you now. Get over it and them, and let it go. You will never be happy if you keep hoping for these guys." The guys stared at Will, who waved them off and stepped through his door. "See y'all later. It was fun."

"If my joy was linked to anything other than what God thought about me, then that will really be a problem for me. Thanks be to God, my Father, for the grace to realize that joy happens as a result of my discovery of the treasure within me; Christ." The pain ripped open afresh in Christian. He was losing his friends because of his passion for Christ, and yet he knew he could be hated because of what he believed and stood for. It didn't feel good though.

Jesus, teach me to be patient and loving, even through the storms. You are my Savior and I am grateful to have given myself entirely to You in love, just as Pastor James taught us today. I love You, precious Lover of my soul, with all my heart, I really do! Amen.

The guys walked quietly after that, until each one made it home. Only time would tell the impact that this day truly had on Christian's friends.

Christian went to bed with his mind on Devin. He had tried calling and texting him a few times with no luck. The

198

voicemail suggested he may have even changed his number. Christian was most concerned about him because every time his mind framed his image in his mind, he had a sick, churning feeling in the pit of his stomach. It was then that he heard the shots ring out, and he knew something really bad had happened to one of his friends.

CHAPTER ELEVEN

News of a shooting in the community was nothing new and it often went unnoticed. It was too common a recurrence for most people in the community to pay attention to it. Isaac heard about Mitch's murder before the other guys did, and it was late in the night when he posted a text asking if it was true that the guys realized that the murder they had heard whispers about happened to be one of them. No one slept after hearing, and they spent the rest of the night and into mid-morning talking and reminiscing. It was heartbreaking, and even when some of the guys met up to pray and try comforting each other, it was difficult to find the words to express just how broken they were. Even Christian was unnaturally silent most of the time.

Everyone in the neighborhood knew what happened. Devin's gang had taken on the other gang in an all-out gun battle a few blocks from where they all usually play basketball. Four young men were left bleeding to death in the quiet streets of Vernon and no one was talking. No one wanted to get involved in the escalating gang war because the peace and safety of their homes and family was of paramount importance to them.

Christian spent a few days reminiscing the contradictions of reality. While salvation was being experienced on one side of town, there was a life and death battle going on simultaneously on the other side. Mitch was supposed to be at church with them that day, but instead, she assumed the family responsibility of going to the supermarket and cooking dinner. The murderers went looking for Devin in retaliation for someone murdered on their side of town but found his sister instead. Everyone knew the truth, but no one was talking to the authorities because they feared for their lives.

Mitch had a wonderful funeral. The First Lady officiated, and Pastor James committed the body. Everyone was there, except Devin. He knew he was blamed for the death of his sister, so he remained unnoticed in a corner of the cemetery and watched the procession and service from a distance. No one knew he was there, though Christian sensed that he must be. He wanted so badly to talk to Devin, to see if he was okay, to pray with him. Devin's choices had finally caught up to him, and Christian knew that retaliation would only make it worse. The entire neighborhood was now under a State of Emergency with soldiers constantly patrolling the area, and no one could get in and out without showing some identification.

Isaac had skyped in during the viewing of the body because he wanted the closure of knowing it was really Mitch. He broke down when he saw her, though she looked at peace. It still hurt that he would not see her again and wished he had paid more attention to her when he had the chance. She was a humble and ambitious soul who only wanted to see her brother assume greater responsibility for his own life. Instead, she became a victim of his selfish path and only confirmed how destructive the emptiness within can become, if left unaddressed. In their hearts, all the friends knew that unless God fills that void within, it can only lead to destruction and death. For the most part, it went unspoken, but the conviction was there. Mitch had her entire life ahead of her. She was supposed to go off to college, get her degree and become a changer of worlds. But instead, she was buried along with all her dreams, aspirations, and ambitions. Whatever her destiny was, it would never see the light of day.

It would be a couple weeks and a few more isolated gang-related incidence before the lives of Christian and his friends saw any form of normalcy.

CHAPTER TWELVE

Three weeks after Mitch's funeral, Thomas initiated a group text. There was a new designer milkshake place opening in town, and the heat had been unbearable. The guys hadn't met up in about a week because of the grief of losing their friend, extreme weather and having only a few options outside of swimming and outdoor recreation.

When they arrived at two in the afternoon, they saw that, once again, they were short another guy. Colton was a no show. They had been to a few youth gatherings, a few of them had gone to the Wednesday night services, and tomorrow was the next Sunday service. Thomas was interested in who might be going, but he didn't want any arguing over text. It seemed clear to a few of the guys that life was dividing them into two groups.

Colton was missing and that visibly bothered Christian, who had mostly kept to himself. He assumed the responsibility of not spending one on one time with Mitch to share the heart of God with her before she died. He was instructed by the Spirit to speak to her many times, but he never did. He always put off talking to her personally for another time and it really bothered him. He didn't know if the love of Christ ignited faith in her or not. Maybe at the last moment, she gave her heart to God. Christian was not sure of one's capacity to think soberly when they are staring down the barrel of a gun, with a murderous intent behind the trigger.

Thomas was ready to talk. He was hoping that the milkshake parlor would provide a place quiet enough for them to speak and heal.

Moments later, Will sat down with his mint-brownie-truffle shake, a sandwich and fries. "Have you guys heard the rumors going around about Devin?" It was like opening an old wound. With all that had transpired, they seemed further away from Devin than ever. Even though a few of them had tried to reach out to him and may have had an unpleasant encounter or two with him on the streets, no one had seemed to connect with him enough to initiate any form of conversation.

Thomas was having the strawberry-banana-fudge shake and answered between digging large strawberries from the side of the glass. "Some. What did you hear?" He didn't make eye contact with his friends, but the cold statement went through the table like a sharp knife cutting the friendly atmosphere.

Christian sipped at his chocolate-truffle shake. Will went on, "I heard he's dealing - and using, and stealing and killing with the other guys in the gang. I guess our guy is a full-timer now, and knowing Devin, he'll for sure try to end up in charge someday. I'm scared for him, he ain't that bad, but he's messing with serious stuff."

Thomas nodded and added, "I heard he's involved in the gang stuff too, but also that he got a girl pregnant. He's going to be a dad, that's heavy stuff. I'm going to commit to praying for him more."

It was obvious that they were all trying to do their best not to talk about his involvement with Mitch's murder.

Will looked around at all of them. "I've had this thought for some time, but it was bad, and I didn't want Colton to blow his crazy gasket like the other night. So, since he's not here, I'm going to say it. I think Devin set up the robbery at the poker game."

AJ dropped a pineapple slice back into his shake. "Are you serious?"

"Think about it. Colton asked me to go, and when I said no, Devin jumped in there. We've only seen him once since then, at the pool party, and he wasn't shaken up like Colton was. I could be wrong; it just seems like they ain't ever had problems until Devin got involved. Seems fishy to me, you don't think?" Will's eyes were cold as he spoke. He was not sure whether he was right or not, but he had given serious thought to it before speaking.

AJ's jaw was hanging open. He shuts it and shook his head. "I never thought about it like that. You're right though. I don't expect we'll ever know the full truth."

Thomas spoke gently, as if he was thinking out loud more than trying to communicate with his friends. "I wouldn't tell Colton."

Will frowned. "What did you say?"

Thomas spoke again, louder this time, "Don't tell Colton. The last thing we need is for the two hotheads to go at it. Especially if he is getting deeply involved with that gang. It could be deadly, and we have already lost a friend to this foolishness. Just keep your mouth shut, yeah?" Thomas was never this forceful when he spoke. One of the changes he was finding since he became a partaker in the life of Jesus was a boost in his self-confidence.

"I got it, man. Take a chill pill." Will couldn't even grin about this right now. He had never seen Thomas get this involved. Part of him liked Thomas' new attitude and another part thought he was taking it a little too far and too soon. He had never said anything like "shut up" to the entire group before.

Christian wanted to move the conversation another way. "If we look into the face of our Maker, we will discover the image and likeness of every man, even those who believe differently from us. In his heart, love flows out for all, even for the most unlikely. As we are busy pointing fingers at each other, competing and comparing ourselves to others, we are missing the moment of enjoying divinity in one another. Humanity is not created for anything less than love. You cannot afford to miss the fullness of life while majoring on the unnecessary. If we could let love live and take away the masks of religion, beliefs, and convictions we have been hiding behind, we would finally begin to accept the beauty of each other and of ourselves. In that moment, we begin to open up our shells of fear and even disarm our defense systems. There would be no need to hide or defend because there would be no-one to challenge. Love would be all that exists and there is no hint of fear in the presence of love."

There was silence for a brief moment, and then Thomas spoke, "That is the most we have heard you say since that day."

The day was when Colton took out his anger on Christian; the same day their friend was being murdered at her home. Christian didn't want Colton's angry attack to define their relationship or influence their conversations. His mission of bringing them all to the awareness of their oneness with Jesus and His infinite love was fulfilling for Christian and his only quest. It made him happy that he was having some success.

AJ said, "Well, what Colton did wasn't cool. How did you feel about that?" His expression was of genuine concern. They had all been worried Christian was really hurt.

Christian shook his head and spoke with an embarrassed laughter. "I don't want to talk about that. What did y'all think of church? We can leave those other incidents alone."

Thomas smiled. He worried about his friends not being able to cope with what life was giving them at the moment, but he was also very excited about the new path he had decided to take, and couldn't stop talking about it. "Man, thanks for inviting us, after all this time of us razzing you and talking garbage. I met Jesus that night and you were telling the truth, that the sense of being empty and void melts like ice in water. I feel happy when I get up, and things still get me down, but I don't accept being unhappy or troubled anymore. Since I started the daily fellowship with Jesus, I understand that His name is a strong tower; I am in Him, He is in me and I am safe. He tells me not to grieve, for His joy is my strength. So, I do not fear, for He is always with me; I will not be dismayed, for He is my savior and salvation. He strengthens me and upholds me with His righteous hand. He has given me victory over the powers and authorities, He defeated them at the cross. I will praise and exalt Him, all the days of my life. Jesus is my refuge when I am oppressed, a stronghold in times of trouble. I lack nothing, because my trust is in Him. He keeps my heart in peace—because I have no other God but Him. I trust in the Lord forever, for in Him I am in the everlasting rock. His presence is with me. He will not fail me or forsake me. He redeemed me from the lies I believed about His Father, Him, His Spirit, and myself. He called me by my name and here's what He said to me: '*You are mine! When you pass through the waters, I will be with you; and through the rivers, they shall not overwhelm you; when you walk through fire, you shall not be burned, and the flame shall not consume you. For I am your Father, the Lover of your being.'* I want to learn everything I can and get to where I can help people know the real Jesus and see Him change their lives too, just like He turned mine around."

Christian nodded on the outside, and on the inside, he was rejoicing. Thomas had not only freely accepted the salvation Jesus provided in him but was also committed to spreading the word. He couldn't have asked for more.

AJ said, "Man, that's so cool!" raising both his hands with closed fists.

Dominic hadn't said a word yet. Will prodded him. "Dominic, what do you think of that? We're the only two *normal* people left at this table."

Dominic responded in a quiet tone. "I want to go tomorrow, if that's okay."

Everyone got excited except Will who was a little confused. AJ, Thomas and especially Christian lit up in big smiles. Dominic continued, "I haven't officially invited Jesus into my heart, but I started talking to Him more after my talk with pastor, after everything that has happened and it's like there's someone in front of me when I start. I always close my eyes, but last night was weird. As I started to talk to Jesus, I felt like I became really open and my heart was like it was on fire. I was crying because I felt a presence in my room, and I couldn't stop talking to Jesus and crying at the same time. I really can't explain it, but something happened that I need to know more about. I woke up really happy and at peace today. Something is different. I want whatever this is, this relationship with Jesus, but I know I got a long way to go."

Christian nearly jumped from his seat in joy. "I'm so happy for everyone. I really am. Dom, it sounds like Jesus wanted you to know that He is real, He was in your room. Also, before thinking about inviting Him in your heart, He had already included you in His Life. Most people think they must invite Jesus into their lives or invite the Spirit into their meetings. The truth is, Jesus is the One who invited us into the eternal fellowship of the Father and the Son. The good news doesn't depend on our invitation but His. If we were able to choose God, then Jesus wouldn't have come. Because we were unable to invite God in our heart, He invited us into His; because we couldn't choose Him, He choose us; we couldn't save ourselves, Jesus saved us; we couldn't redeem ourselves, Jesus delivered and redeemed us. Once lost; all found, safe and sound. It's all about Jesus' person and work, not ours. Regarding the Spirit of God, He is always present where we are. Remember, where two or three are fellowshipping, Jesus is present with His Father and the Spirit. We try so hard to feel His presence because we are simply disconnected in our own minds from the consciousness of our oneness with the Godhead. This is the great awakening: '*My son, you have always been with Me and all that I have is yours!*' He's always been there, He wanted you to feel His sweet touch. It's just amazing, I have those moments sometimes and I'm telling you, it's something we can't fully explain. Will, are you coming tomorrow as well? At least you can have fun with a bunch of people."

Christian may have lost Colton as a friend, but he had joy that three of his friends had become partakers of the nature and character of Christ within. The Spirit of wisdom did it and his willingness to share the gospel of love and grace with anyone who didn't know the heart of God. He felt awesome but was also humbled to tears. He wanted to see all his friends come to enjoy the salvation in Christ. He would not stop praying until they were all enjoying God as their very own Father and Lover. Christian was afraid to reach out to Devin now especially, but it was because of his hatred for Jesus, not Christian.

The guys joked around for a little longer and studied the other shake flavors, deciding which they would try on their next visit.

There was a brief moment of silence as each of the friends thought of the missing four. Devin was a lost cause to some, but they would keep praying. Colton was missing in action and no one seemed to know where he is or what he had been up to lately. Mitch was gone, and all they had left of her were memories. Isaac was trying to enjoy his time in Europe, but he missed his friends. He had engaged a few of them in a private conversation, getting updates and sharing pictures of their journeys. Christian was happy for the four he was sharing this moment with, and they were grateful for him sticking around when they really wanted to get rid of him because of the changes in his life. They now see Christian in a different light, and while the pain of loss and change still stung at their hearts, there was also peace and a sense of joy that life extended beyond their troubled community, and they had hope.

Christian went home and dropped to his knees praying for guidance. *"Precious Lord Jesus Christ, beloved of the Father, eternal and faithful Son of God. Please share Your knowledge of the Father's heart with me, so that I may know and live a life that will reflect the beauty of Your life in me. Come into my deepest fears and brokenness with Your light. Search out my blindness and share Your unearthly assurance with me in areas of my heart and mind where fears hold me captive. Find all my broken parts and bathe them with Your Father's love. Allow my soul to be continuously baptize with Your peace so that I may be guided and inspired by You in everything I do. In Christ I pray, Amen."*

Christian needed God to direct his steps, that he would not be doing anything in vain. After he committed to love the Lord and had his path directed by the love God gave to all His children, he knew what his call was. He felt a strong desire to invite more people to what he had experienced. He knew the love of Jesus alone called people to walk into church, but spreading the word was really working out for him. He was overwhelmed by happiness but there was also a strange feeling of discomfort. Darkness was brewing in a secret corner somewhere and it was about to reveal its ugly head. He thought about Devin. He won't give up on his friend's awakening to the love of Jesus, not now; not ever. He can be saved too. Christian picked up his phone dialed a very familiar number. It rang and just when it seemed like the voicemail was going to pick up as usual, he heard, "Hey, what do you want?"

"Devin? I was, uh… I just wanted to say hi, and umm, I'm sorry about your sister and, umm, I wanted to see how you were doing."

"Dude, we aren't chicks. We don't need to gab and check in."

Devin sounded mean on the phone and Christian almost regretted calling. But he chose not to give up on Devin. "I get that, I just wanted to remind you that my invitation is always open. Like my door, if you need a friend. I would love to hang out, anytime…"

Devin cut in loudly, his tone fierce. "Are you serious? Did you call to push your Jesus stuff on me? Dude, you need the kinda help even Jesus can't give you. Leave it alone and leave me alone. Don't bother me with that crap again. You need weed or wanna have a real fun time, then you call me. Not one minute before that, you get it?"

Christian was stunned into silence. He wanted to say something but couldn't find any words. Devin started laughing and made sure Christian heard him tell whoever was around, "This cat is crazy," before he hung up the phone.

Christian didn't expect an apology during the phone call or warm fuzzy feelings, but he didn't expect that either. He was crushed, but he knew he was acting out of love for his friends, and just wanted all of them to be partakers of the divine nature of Christ Jesus.

His phone rang and he picked it up without looking at it, hoping Devin had a change of heart.

"Hey man, I'm really sorry about what I did a couple weeks ago and not being around. Can you meet me so we can talk?"

Christian smiled, feeling better and worse all at the same time, "Sure Colton, text me. I'll be there."

CHAPTER THIRTEEN

Christian showed up a little nervous and a little anxious at JoJo's Pizza Joint. He was not exactly afraid, but worried about what could happen. What if this turned ugly?

Colton was waiting for him and said hello first. He didn't look angry. "Hey, I'm glad you actually came."

It made Christian relax a little. "Why wouldn't I?"

"What happened was wrong, and I wanted to apologize in person. You deserve that." Colton seemed different to Christian. The apology was so easy and free, and he seemed genuinely sorry for his bad behavior.

Christian smiled back and said, "I appreciate that, man. More than you know. You're forgiven, we're cool." Colton seemed willing to make amends and this could lead to having his friend back and free to enjoy the knowledge of Christ together. They ordered a medium meat-lovers pizza and a bottle of pepsi.

"Pastor James invited me out to watch a NBA game the other night. It was so cool. The First Lady was also there, and I saw a different side to them. They were normal people, just like me and you. Afterwards, Pastor talked to me for a while. He even made sure I got a ride home." Colton looked at his feet and seemed to try and avoid making eye contact. It made him look like a big puppy, knowing he did something wrong and regretting it.

"He's a good guy, really, he is. They are both good people." Christian didn't want to ask a ton of questions. Colton needed to keep talking and not shut down.

Colton finally raised his head. He smiled and said, "I also wanted to thank you."

Christian looked a little taken aback. "For what?"

"Pastor James took me through the Bible and showed me everything you've been saying to us. It also helped me to see what a good friend you really are, to care for us the way you do. You never gave up on us. You're really a model to look up to. You're my hero. I will always tell my story and will mention you in it. I love you, Christian." Colton's face was covered with tears. His voice trembled a little and his hands were shaky. He had rehearsed these words and he meant them.

Christian hated that he always seemed to be close to tears with these things. His heart had changed so much. When he opened up to be led by Jesus, he became open to the way he felt and to how other people felt. He considered everyone a brother or sister now and it left him feeling their emotions. But he made a strong effort not to choke up. While eating, Colton shared all the notes he took during the discussion with Pastor James, Christian enjoyed every single part of it, and they had such a great time together.

"Hey Chris, I was talking to my neighbor about all these things I just told you and she was so blessed."

"Oh yeah?"

"Yes, she asked me if I could talk to her kids about Jesus. I guess because she is seeing the change in me and wants the same for her children as well." Colton had been sharing the love of God with the people around him.

"Congratulations, that's amazing. I am very proud of you. What shall it profit us to live within the confines of religion and yet lose relationship with those close to us?" Christian was sincerely thanking Jesus for expressing Himself through his friend.

"Absolutely nothing! Wonderful. You always have an inspired word when we talk. I love you, my friend." Colton was feeling blessed and thankful to God for the meeting with Christian.

"You know, I love you too. By the way, regarding going around trying to preach, I don't really plan to preach to anyone when I wake up every morning, I simply love on everyone around me and the testimonies follow. I understood that at the end of the day, it's a blessing to be excluded for who I include, than to be included for who I exclude. The Gospel is a love letter to all, because all have been included and all are invited at the table to feast with Father, Son and Holy Spirit." Christian was very caring.

He didn't want his friend to continue to be open to all types of people, races, religion, ethnicities, etc…

He invited Colton to a special event and a swimming party. He wanted to change the subject away from himself, but still talked about church. He grew up without someone inviting him to cool places and wanted to do it differently for Colton.

Christian was an orphan and even though he hated that word, he knew very well what it meant. His journey to where he was now had been full of pain and loss. He once thought he would stay with his grandparents until he was an adult - but then grandpa died, and grandma ended up in a nursing home.

Christian was all alone at a young age and shipped off to a stranger's house. It had seemed like hell. While he was at the foster home, he used to think that at least the other kids had parents who might come get them when they got out of jail or off drugs or fixed whatever it was that had gone wrong in their lives. Those kids had the chance of somewhere else to go but Christian didn't. He had lived so long being sad and lonely. Even now, he remembered the anger all too well.

Then his foster family took him to church. He didn't want to go. He felt forced. But as soon as he started paying attention to what Pastor James was saying, he changed. God quickly became Christian's only love, just as a loving father with his son. If someone had told him then that his friends would start to change because of his obedience, he would not have believed it. But after enduring all the negativity, loss, fear, death, and anger around and inside him, he had become a light in his friends' lives and community, nothing filled him with more joy.

§

It was a special night. Christian didn't know if the guys had seen it announced but after service there was a special event happening, then a swimming party. All the guys knew they were supposed to bring their trunks.

They met up for church. Pastor James took the stage right after worship and announced the surprise baptism after service. They were going to take Communion, and then commence the baptism service.

Pastor James quieted the bunch. "Praise God, precious family in Christ. We do celebrate baptisms here. I am going to take the time to explain what true baptism is and why we also practice water baptism from time to time when people request for it after realizing that Jesus gave Himself in love for them, forgiving their trespasses and immersed them into His shared life with His Father and Holy Spirit."

Somebody in the crowd started the applause. Pastor James nodded in agreement and started again. "Ephesians 4:4-6 says, 'There is one body and one Spirit, just as you were called to one hope when you were called; one Lord, one faith, ***one baptism***; one God and Father of all, who is over all and through all and in all.' Since there are different baptisms referred to in the New Testament, it can be a bit confusing when we read about one baptism. The word *baptize* always means to submerge or immerse. So, when baptism is discussed, it involves a person being totally submerged into something else. Baptism implies being all in. It also implies that a change has taken place. Baptized people are changed people. Generally speaking, there are two types of baptism: a physical (water) baptism performed by John the Baptist and a spiritual baptism. One is literal, done in water by a man; the other is figurative, accomplished in the spirit realm by the Spirit. The one true baptism is the one that the Spirit does. There is a notion about baptism that has been preached for generations now, which is: you must be baptized in water to be saved. Now, if you haven't heard this, that's actually great news. If you want to hear it, you can simply travel a few miles and you will find a religious group that is going to say: 'Man, it's great that you believe in Jesus Christ, but… It's amazing that you have accepted the gospel message, but… Remember, two thousand years ago, there were people coming behind Paul the apostle and saying Paul's message is great, but, you need to be circumcised. People always thought that we need to do something physical to make sure that we are truly right with God. Of course, Paul got really upset about that, totally frustrated with the Galatians for believing so easily in such ideologies. There will always be people who will twist the good news. The equation most religion will offer you regarding this particular subject will usually be: Jesus Christ + concussion = salvation. This isn't the right equation from God. Ephesians 2:8 says, *'For it is by grace you have been saved, through faith—and this is not from yourselves, it is the gift of God.'* Grace reveals who you are, and the faith of God persuades you of it. So, be careful about what you expose your ears and hearts to. So please, if you used to think that you are only okay with God if you're immersed in the water, then try to adjust that notion. Paul will be furious about this notion today, just like he was when he was still on earth. Let's take a look at 1 Corinthians 1:13-16 - Paul asked the following questions: Can Christ be cut up into little relics? Was Paul crucified for you? Were you baptized into Paul's name? He continued by telling them that water Baptism isn't his business or emphasis; that he was actually glad that he only baptized Crispus, Gaius and the family of Stephanus. Somehow, baptism in water has become a snare to some who wish to win members to their denomination. He who didn't need to be baptized, was vicariously baptized for us and as us. In Jesus' baptism, the world was baptized, for He is the last Adam who vicariously represents the entire human race. Isn't it weird that we easily believe that whatever happened to the first Adam happened to all of us? Why don't we believe that everything that happened to the Lord of all equally happened to us? Is Adam a greater destroyer than Jesus a greater Savior? Jesus is greater than Adam. Adam is a human being and Jesus is the Creator of all things, visible and invisible. So, everything that occurred during Jesus Christ' birth, life, baptism, crucifixion, death, resurrection, ascension and seating at the Father's right hand, affected the entire human race to a far much greater degree, far beyond what happened to men in Adam. So Paul baptized five to six people max. Knowing the influence of Paul in the ministration of the gospel, don't you think what is preached today about water baptism is a little concerning?"

The entire church was quiet, and Pastor James had the attention of everyone in the room. Even the instrument ministers who were sometimes thinking about their next play weren't talking but focused and open to hear the voice of the heart of God through Pastor James.

"Paul tells us in 1 Corinthians 15:10 '*I worked harder than all of them--yet not I, but the grace of God that was with me.*' For Paul to say that he worked more than all the others and throughout his ministry, he only baptized the amount of people he mentioned… that should indicate to us that being baptized in water does not save us; faith in the finished work of Christ does. You can read Ephesians 2:8-9 and Romans 10:9. Peter and John baptized three thousand people in one day, according to Acts 2:41 '*Those who accepted his message were baptized, and about three thousand were added to their number that day.*' But, how could Paul say that he worked more than the others while their number of baptisms in one day was well over what he did in his entire lifetime? The answer to that question is found in verse 17 of 1 Corinthians 1 *'For Christ did not send me to baptize, but to preach the gospel.'* Paul is literally telling us that his mandate was not about winning members for some 'Christian group' through baptism. But he was commissioned to declare the good news without any strings attached; nothing to distract from the powerful effect of the revelation of the cross of Christ. The mystery of the cross is the revelation of man's inclusion in the death and resurrection of Jesus Christ. The good news is the powerful rescuing act of God that persuades both Jew and Gentile alike."

The leaders jumped and started praising God. Pastor James turned, looked at his wife and saw that her eyes were closed. She was praying for him throughout the preaching so people who were in the building, and those watching on livestream, would experience the life changing power of God through the message he was preaching. He turned and continued. "This good news reveals how God rescued the life of our design and redeemed our original identity. Mankind would never again be judged righteous or unrighteous by their own ability to obey moral laws. It is not about what we must or must not do but about what Jesus has already done for us and as us. Do you know that even Jesus didn't baptize people?" The entire crowd looked at Pastor James, waiting to hear his next statement. "He didn't. John 3:22 says, "*After this, Jesus and his disciples went out into the Judean countryside, where he spent some time with them, and baptized.*" John 4:2 says, "*Although in fact it was not Jesus who baptized, but his disciples.*" Given the proximity of the two verses, John meant that Jesus was with His disciples, while His disciples were baptizing people in John 3:22, and that Jesus Himself was not baptizing people. Again, the work of Jesus wasn't to baptize in water, because that wasn't what man needed. Here are the words of John the Baptist in Matthew 3:11, '*I baptize you with water for repentance. But after me comes **one who is more powerful than I.** He will baptize you with the Holy Spirit and fire.*' Don't think I am saying we don't celebrate being immersed in water; we do because through water baptism we celebrate our union with Christ in His death. The act of being voluntarily immersed in water is your choice; thus, a public proclamation of your testimony of having been born again by the grace of God."

Pastor James's voice was uplifting but firm. He sounded excited to say the Word of the Lord and he was clearly a very knowledgeable man. There was more cheering. Will looked around and saw the joy in the people around him. He noticed that some people had tears in their eyes. "There is no person with whom Jesus does not stand. Not one person! Against every hurled accusation, every derision and all that mocks our existence; famine, decay, murder, disaster, disease and death, Jesus has our back. Always. He does this as our human brother and as God. We can't escape being human. The honest believers admit there is no ultimate security in our Bible, our statements of belief, our systems, our sometimes brilliant, often frail human leaders, past or present, or in locating the most ancient, orthodox, or faithful church. We can't escape trust. We can't escape leaning against a bitter wind. We can't escape the chasm between faith and seeing what is promised by God. There is instead an existential uncertainty that leads us to the manger and the cross and the empty tomb and the upper room where, in each place, the faithfulness of Jesus Christ is all we find and—in the end, thanks be to God—all we need. God is human, and we are not human until we are human as God is human in the moment the flesh of Jesus is nailed to the tree of life—that is when we finally become human—what you might call a crystalline joy, an anticipation and a reminder that resurrection is the end of all things and not death."

Once again there was clapping and cheering. Will couldn't help but think this was like some of the movies he watched—the high drama, Jesus dying for his sins. Why would somebody do that? It seemed silly, really. No one was perfect, so what was the point of dying so we could all mess up all the time?

Pastor James seemed to single him out. Pastor continued his explanation, but Will felt his words as though he was talking straight to him. "Jesus took care of all your mess as well, and yours, and yours, and yours, and mine. Why? Because we are all a part of this world. So, from God's point of view, you're forgiven because Jesus took away the sins of the world and you are now right with God. Forgiveness is 'once for all' or nothing at all. Any middle ground is an insult to the person and work of Jesus Christ." Pastor James looked at his wife again and noticed that she was coming towards him.

"I have a word from the Father."

"Sure, my dear." She took the mic and started speaking.

"I will greatly advantage you by giving My laws in your hearts and engrave them in your inmost thoughts. I have deleted the record of your sins and misdeeds. I no longer recall them. Says the Father and Lover of the human race!" Her voice was shaking just like her entire body. She gave back the mic to Pastor James.

"Abba Father, we are so grateful. You are such an amazing Dad to each one of us and we can't thank You enough for all You did for us in Christ by Your Spirit. You all better be louder about that than anything else you've heard." Everyone was repeating after Pastor James. Some people couldn't stop thanking God through laughter, words and dances. There was such a sweet and heavy presence of the Spirit of joy on everyone in the auditorium. "I'm going to give you a couple more minutes to give Him the praise and glory He deserves. He gave you

His righteousness and took your sins; He took away feelings like depression, rejection, misery, sadness, loneliness and turned them into happiness, inclusion, joy, and acceptance. You all better be dancing right now. He loved you, He loves you and will forever love you!"

During the praise break, Will felt a tugging inside. He was sure that whatever this weight was, it meant something important. There was a torrent of new feelings and he knew it was meant to break the contradictions he had been feeling all this time. He knew the Pastor was talking to him all this time and he realized he was about to be faced with a life-defining decision. He didn't know if he was ready to follow the others for the act of water baptism. But he felt he was doing the right thing, listening to the kind of calling he felt within.

Pastor James continued to a silent and attentive crowd. "Before we go to the water, remember that the act of water baptism pictures how we were buried together with Jesus in his death; then raised together with Him into a new lifestyle. We were like seeds planted together in the same soil, to be quickened together to life. If we were included in Jesus' death, we were equally included in His resurrection. Our old lifestyle was crucified together with Him, and this concludes that the vehicle that accommodated sin in us was discard and rendered entirely useless. Our slavery to sin came to an end. If nothing else stops us from doing something wrong, death certainly does. Some people are asking themselves what the big deal is. I'm so glad you asked!"

There was light laughter from the audience.

"If you join us in this practice today, it would be great. But again, this doesn't bring you closer to God than you already are, and it doesn't make you something you are not yet. It's simply a public statement of what you already think and know about yourself. You are God's child! For we are all baptized by one Spirit to form one body—whether Jews or Gentiles, slave or free—and we were all given the one Spirit to drink. Baptism or immersion, whichever you prefer to call it, in Christ was performed by the Spirit of God only. This took place over two thousand years ago. Do not hesitate! 'By our baptism, then, we were buried with him and shared his death, just as Christ was raised from death by the glorious power of the Father, so also we might live a new life.'"

Pastor James came down off the stage and started walking towards the door with a big smile on his face. His pace was steady, his eyes moving over each face in the first row as he walked down the center alley.

Will looked at his friends. No one was moving but they were all clapping. Everyone else was also clapping and chanting, standing to leave behind the Pastor. This was a surreal scene from a surreal story to Will; it couldn't be happening, it felt like they were all compelled to follow wherever he went. But the strangest thing of all was that he felt the same calling in his gut and started moving along with the cheering crowd.

It was nothing surreal, it was a very common practice. In the summer, Pastor James used the stream that flowed to the river. He appeared stately as he looked around at the group gathering to watch the outdoor water baptism. He stepped closer to the stream and the people followed, listening to his every word. Pastor stood on a monticule carpeted in green grass, with his back to the river and facing the eager crowd.

"The ability to live the life that fulfills your God-given purpose is empowered by Jesus' success at the cross. Again, understand, baptism doesn't make you a member of God's family. Only faith in God-in-Christ does. Baptism is like a wedding ring. It's the visible reminder that you are engaged in a relationship with someone, *in this case it will be* Father, Son, and Holy Spirit. It is not something you put off until you are spiritually mature— that's like waiting until you have enough money to have kids, it ain't ever going to happen—you have to dive right in or else you will always find an excuse."

Will could tell by the crowd's response that some people already knew that was true. They groaned. Other people booed their answer. Their generation was all too aware of how life was harder or so it seems.

Although he was making a big effort and people had followed him to the riverside, Pastor James could tell he was losing a few people's attention. "I'm done guys, I promise. This is a big deal."

Pastor was now standing in the river, ready to receive those who would make the choice to be baptized. First Lady was on the shore, beckoning. "Now, who's ready to get this baptism started?"

The pastor's arms were in the air inviting people in with his hands. The crowd responded with respectful clapping this time.

The guys took part in the Eucharist, the Christian ceremony commemorating the Last Supper, in which bread and wine were consecrated and consumed. When it was done, and while they were walking down to the water, Will came from the sidelines and said to First Lady, "I want to do it too, not because I am a stranger to Abba Father, but because I am a member of the family. I also wanted to thank you and your husband for the amazing messages you shared with us. I have learned a lot and decided voluntarily to be baptize in water today, because I am already in union with God, not because I want to be."

"You are very welcome my dear beloved brother. We are always honored to be able to share the good news." First Lady always made use of every opportunity to share the heart of God with anyone and anywhere.

Will's friends were surprised but also really pleased to see him joining them on this journey of exploring and enjoying the relationship between Father, Son, and Holy Spirit. No one else there knew the internal affairs leading up to this point and why it was such a special move, but there was laughter all around as they were all cheering for Will.

Pastor James started baptizing and did hundreds of people, then came Will's turn. Pastor James prayed, immersed him in the water and said the same words He said for all the others. "You are loved, acquitted, forgiven, adopted, grafted in, restored, redeemed, renewed, dead and resurrected, filled, anointed, perfected, accepted in the beloved, in union with Father, Son and Holy Spirit, destined for glory, sanctified, holy and seated in heavenly places. Enjoy as much as you can this amazing journey you are on with Father, Jesus and Holy Spirit."

When Will came up out of the water, everyone was clapping and cheering, including his friends.

Will looked at them, eyes sparkling and said, "It's oooonnnn. Let us reach our generation, guys. Everybody should be able to feel this. It's amazing! Let us be the sons that allow God to love all men through us."

Pastor James had said, "Once you have a genuine encounter with the real Jesus, the experience completely changes your life," but Will didn't know it was going to be this deep. He was overthrown and overwhelmed, flooded with a fresh stream of love that came straight from the heart of Jesus. He knew this was a day he was not going to forget during his entire life, and it was time to start helping others get out of the chains of darkness they were stuck in.

The day ended beautifully with the swimming party. There was music, food, and fellowship that made the moment so perfect that the guys found themselves not thinking about their past negative experiences. Each of them was enjoying the peace and joy that salvation brought to those who partake, and they were flabbergasted that Christian was telling them this very thing all along, and they were annoyed by it. Were they so blinded to not see? The changes in the guys began to filter into their home lives, and often left their parents speechless and confused about their new behaviors. It was so profound that little Marc and Karen started visiting the church with Dominic. AJ's mom and Dad visited once, and experienced a touch from Jesus the deliverer, through the gospel preached with love and power by Pastor and First Lady and the laying on of hands for their freedom from their addictions. They were a little embarrassed and nervous to go back, because they ended up on the ground while they were being ministered to.

Will couldn't get out of his room sometimes because he wanted to know Jesus more. One night, while reading the epistle of Paul to the Ephesians chapter 1, He could hear a voice talking to him while he was seated at the table in his room where he usually had his Bible and book notes. Will heard during that unique moment while fellowshipping with God, *"Before the foundation of the world, I knew I would enter time, space and become You-Man and die humanity's death once and for all. I made you so that we enjoy each other in all eternity. Before Adam was, I knew I was going to become man, eternally in the person of Jesus. You-man, from the very ground up, have been designed to be fully compatible with me. I was not any less God when I became the man, Jesus. And I am not any less in and through you. Stop looking at your humanity as a negative thing. Stop looking down on yourselves; you are valuable to Me. Do not speak poorly of yourselves, you are in My image. Your humanity is the best idea I ever had. If it wasn't, you wouldn't have been here with Me today. You are 100% compatible with Me, I have shared My all with you. You are filled full of the Spirit without any need for measuring. You are my previous son."*

When Will opened his eyes, he started to thank the Father for the word he just received. At first, he didn't understand what just happened to him, but he could tell that it wasn't anything normal or natural. He had tears all over his face and the only thing he wanted to do was call his friends and tell them what was happening to him during moments of communion with the Godhead. The time he spent trying to satisfy his desire with TV or anything else had come to an end. He felt it, and it felt awesome.

Isaac sat on a canoe on the Viking River. The Guide was directing them to the different attractions as they floated by, but Isaac was preoccupied with his phone. He was scanning through numerous pictures sent to him by the guys. He saw pictures of their baptisms, pictures of them participating in different community services and programs, group pictures with smiling, glowing faces, and numerous, mostly hilarious selfies. Isaac was teary-eyed when he saw the pictures taken of a small ceremony done by the guys where they erected a small monument in memory of Mitch. Someone had painted an almost replica picture of her, and it was signed by all the guys, except Devin, with a space waiting for Isaac's signature. The moment was surreal but there were reasons to be grateful and Isaac was anxious to get back home to his friends.

The Boss sent for Devin. He knew this was his moment to prove himself. He knew he would be given an assignment that would push him a few notches up in his quest for prominence. He had graduated from just knocking people out but taking lives and doing what was required to stay on the Boss's favored radar. In less than a year, he had done what his father took ten years to accomplish, and he was just one assignment away from being promoted. He lost his sister, and he managed to drown his grief by abusing the substance he pushed, so even that incident accelerated his progress because of the repercussions that followed. His gang was now the prominent gang in the community, and he was enjoying the respect that he demanded. Excitement was bubbling up in Devin's stomach as he reached for the doorknob that would take him before the Boss. He had finally made it.

CHAPTER FOURTEEN

"*P*lease don't hurt anyone else." Christian pleaded again with Devin.

Devin's head reeled. He didn't lower the gun but looked straight into his old friend's eyes. They were at complete peace. But his, he knew, were shiny and ready to pour a sea of angry tears. *Why wasn't Christian begging for his life?* The calmness, the acceptance – it undermined Devin's confidence, and took him places he didn't want to go. *How much inner peace did Christian really feel if he didn't seem panicked at all?* He just asked that no one else suffered.

It was a kind of peace Devin would have liked to experience. It seemed a blissful way to live. For a second more, he thought of the air being split by the bullet, the flare from the muzzle and Christian's life ending like a candle flame snuffed out in the wind. But he couldn't do it. It was wrong. It was not the correct path.

Devin felt something inside him break. It was like a covering pulled off his new life, showing it for the evil thing it was. Christian didn't deserve to take a bullet for it, and the future didn't matter. He had done nothing wrong.

Devin lowered the gun, then slipped it back into his waistband and looked at Christian again, tears unshed in his eyes. There was one more smile for his friend, whose life he just could not take, and he headed for the window. He scrambled down the trellis, ruining the flowers, filled with a mix of regret, confusion and joy he couldn't explain. He was defeated and triumphant at the same time.

Boss pulled the car up next to him. "Get in."

Devin jumped in. "I couldn't do it, Boss, I just couldn't. He didn't deserve that bullet. He offered his life to save others."

"We know. Sit back." Big Dog had slid right behind Devin. He trained a gun on the back of his neck as they drove. Devin felt it and understood what was coming. He looked down, trying to control his breathing, staring at his brand-new kicks. Thoughts of imminent death flooded Devin's mind. *What did it feel like to be shot?* He had watched so many bleed out until they could no longer breathe. It didn't always look painful, but the look in their eyes that they would no longer see light was hard to wipe from one's memory.

When they got back to headquarters, Boss walked Devin into the house. He pushed him into the middle of the room and stared him down. Big Dog leaned against the door, watching. Devin stood still, trying not to look either of them in the eye, thinking about another way out.

Big Dog was blocking the only door of escape, and now Boss had a baseball bat in his hands.

The first blow blinded Devin with pain and it was then that memories from his past begun flooding into his mind. He heard the voices of everyone who tried to encourage him to take another path; voices he scuffed at; voices he never had any intention of hearing.

"I'm your sister, Devin. You say you're doing this for me, but it's all about you. If you really cared about me, you would not be doing this." For a moment, Devin felt like Mitch was still alive; as if in that moment, she was watching with teary eyes and regret in her heart.

The second and third hit put Devin on the floor, broken and bleeding. Boss was yelling now, holding nothing back.

"Thought we were fam, man! You chose someone over yo' boys! Mr. Holy got a second chance, but you won't, Devin! You messed up, bruh!"

The words sunk deep, but the memories were more unbearable than the baseball bat crashing against his body and skull.

"There's a way that seems right to a man, but the end thereof is destruction..."

"There is another way..."

"Jesus is the way the truth and the life. He can help you. The void can only be filled by Him."

The memories kept coming until it became analgesia. Flashes from his life was random with each hit that his body took. He could hear his bones breaking, tasted blood curdling in his mouth and his lungs tighten, making it harder to breathe, but his memory; his soul remained untouched. He saw his youth; the innocence in his eyes when he played in the backyard with Mitch. They didn't have a care in the world, but only knew what it meant to just be a human being. Life had potential, unlimited possibilities. Devin told his sister that when he grew up, he wanted to be a Airline Pilot. Mitch wanted to be a soldier and help defend her family against bad people.

Devin was conscious while trying to shield himself, but Big Dog's boots joined in, landing on his back. Devin couldn't see it, but he knew Big Dog had that gun on him. He was still able to see, though blood was flowing in his eyes, but he couldn't move. The slightest attempt sent excruciating pain throughout his entire body. He could feel his life slowly draining away, the light that made reality possible to see was slowly dimming and the thought of whether there was anything beyond was tormenting. In that moment, Devin understood that if the void is filled with anger, selfishness and greed, there could be nothing but destruction. Even those responsible for taking his life were also victims of the emptiness. They needed God as much as he did, but it was too late now for him to make that decision.

"Somebody is dying tonight, Devin, and you chose wrong. You gonna be an example, boy. The next soldier who thinks he tough enough and bows out like you did, he gon' think twice because you're gonna remind them we ain't playing!"

Devin couldn't breathe. He could barely keep his eyes open as a few more kicks landed in his ribs. He barely felt the kicks as he felt surreal, as if he was now standing outside of his body watching himself die. The scene was devoid of light, but still visible, like a dream.

Boss was laughing as he noticed Devin's eyes begin to twitch and close. "Don't fall asleep on me. I got one last thing for you. Look at me, kiddo."

Devin couldn't move his head. The blood was thick in his mouth.

"He's already dead, Boss. No one can survive that."

"I ain't taking no chance."

Boss raised the gun, and flashed a grin, teeth white in the darkness.

"Time's up."

Boss pulled the trigger seven times.

Devin's final memory was with him and his friends playing basketball.

"I wish you'd all just shut up about this stupid emptiness talk. There's no such thing as a void. We create our own destiny. We make our own path. We decide our life's fate."

TO BE CONTINUED...

EPILOGUE

In *The Void*, Alain Lea has touched the fundamental nerve within the human heart – the need and desire to believe that we matter. There is a thirst to know that our lives serve a greater purpose than to drink from the shallow waters of pleasure, position and possessions until the clock runs out and the game is over in this world. This novel has spoken to the reader at a level deeper than the mind. It has done more than entertain or even inspire. It has *informed* through sharing the stories of eight individual characters with one common need – to discover the life Christian knows and effortlessly expresses. *The Void* has led the reader to the One who fills the perceived Void that can only be filled by Divine Love.

These characters are a microcosm of humanity as a whole. In some way, each one is you and me. We all live inside our respective cultures based on location, assets, education, race, age, and other variables that distinguish us and yet the underlying need we all share is to be loved and to express love. Alain Lea has creatively taken us by the arm and led us to the Source of love we all seek. As you lay this book down, don't lay down its message. Pick up and put on the Divine Love you have experienced in these pages.

This book is a story but there is a greater story, one that will be told in eternity. It is your story, your life. Today can be the beginning of a new chapter for you. Simply open the pages of your life to the One whom Scripture calls the *Author* and *Finisher* of faith. Allow Him to complete the story which is your life. You may be living in an early chapter or near the closing chapter of life. Wherever you find yourself in the wonderful narrative your Creator has designed for you, the story becomes better and better. So, live out your own story as Christian did with confidence that when "time's up" in this world, yours will have been a wonderful tale of divine love expressed through your daily life.

Dr. Steve McVey
Best-Selling Author

THE VOID II

The reality is like the end of this story, which will be answered in the next volume: Time can be up without any warning. I am urging you today, by the compassion of Christ, to answer God's invitation to meet them in your soul. If you know you are not partaking yet of the life of God within you, and you really want to by having a true relationship with the Father through Jesus by the assistance of sweet Holy Spirit, NOW is the time. You can say this prayer:

Dear Father, in the freedom of Your endless love and in the safety of Your divine embrace, I acknowledge that Jesus Christ is Your Eternal Son. I got lost in my own darkness, instead of living in Your joy. I got crippled inside. Instead of receiving Your love, my soul was disturbed. Today, I acknowledge and believe that the life of Jesus from His birth to His seating at the right hand of God was vicarious. I was co-crucified with Jesus, I co-died on the cross with Him; I was co-buried together with Him; on the third day I co-raised from among the dead with Him; I co-ascended on

> *high with Jesus and I am co-seated at Your right hand with Him as well. I acknowledge in my heart and agree to the fact that Jesus Christ is Lord of all and over all. I give myself in love to You today, just as You gave yourself in love for me and to me. Here I am Father, Jesus and Holy Spirit, LOVE me. Amen!*

If you sincerely repeated these words, I want to congratulate you. Welcome back home!

The Father God welcomes you and celebrates your return to the consciousness of your true identity. You are a partaker of the saving work and life of Jesus Christ. The journey of love and discovery has started. It is important for you to continuously grow in the knowledge of the love, the person and finished work of Jesus Christ by allowing your soul to be fed with the words of grace. For you have been crucified with Christ, it is no longer you who live, but Christ lives in you. Therefore, the terms co-crucified and alive together with Christ defines you now. Christ in you and you in Him. It is a blessing to know that the life you live is entirely by the faith of another (Jesus Christ), so you have nothing to worry about from now on. He got your back from start to finish. Live your life overwhelmed by God's opinion of you.

I advise you to find a Christo-centric local church to learn more about Jesus, His Father and Holy Spirit; then you will discover who you really are and what already belongs to you by virtue of your origin and identity. Celebrate who you already are in God's family every single day of your life. *You matter to God!*

MORE PRAISES FOR THE VOID

I highly recommend this book for those who are tired of doing the same things repeatedly and expecting different results and to those desiring to discover how to connect with the real life within. The experience of this read will certainly help to release the experience of the I AM. This novel is a worthwhile read, which is absolutely "cutting edge" and revolutionary in its approach to present truth. It will open the reader to an awareness of the "NOW" which is vital to true spiritual understanding. The Scripture records that, "Hope deferred makes the heart sick" (See Proverbs 13:12). So many people today have become confused and discouraged by futuristic thinking. This novel will definitely help you become aware of "now" and that today is the day of salvation. Enjoy the different layers contained herein as you come to know that AWARENESS IS EXPERIENCE!

Many today do not realize the difference between knowing ABOUT Christ and truly KNOWING Him as their daily experience and walk. This novel was written in a clear and concise manner, revealing a fresh realization from a higher perspective than many Christian writings of our day. Enjoy this awesome read and experience the true author of life.

Dr. Kay Fairchild
President and Founder of New Life Ministries, USA

The Void! This is such a masterpiece which goes deep to highlight the struggle of many young people today in our society. The author uses simplicity to bring to clarity the deep hidden Void which drives lots of our young people from one lifestyle to another, trying to satisfy this Void in themselves. In this narrative, you will discover the simplicity that is in the gospel of Christ and how religion has succeeded in keeping many people away from the God-life with lots of lies. You will see how God has reconciled himself to humanity, yet people still feel they are distant from Him. Distance is an illusion; it is not real, as propagated through religion. There is life so real out there in Christ, life which goes on and on and on and awaits you to exploit. Alain Lea brings into clarity what God has always had in mind for mankind. You will be greatly enriched through this masterpiece, well-crafted through the inspiration of the Holy Spirit. Read it and pass it on.

Pastor Bonface Odhiambo
Grace Family Chapel, Nairobi Kenya

§

What a powerful, insightful and relational book. Reading it will cause many like the prodigal son to come to themselves and cause them to realize that God loves them so much and has a great purpose for their lives.

The Void is a must read for many thousands that go through life struggling with depression, rejection, misery and often times go through life with the agony and pain of hopelessness.

Dr. Alain Lea, with the help of the Holy Spirit, will cause many who will read this piece of manuscript to come to the knowledge of God and His everlasting love. It is a timely book in that it has come in such a time as this, with a generation of millions of men, women and youths struggling with depression, addictions and many harmful habits that are caused by one feeling "empty."

Glory be to God for such a timely book. I see it bringing salvation to many generations to come.

Prophetess Chimwemwe Veronica Kaluwa
Founder of the Beauty and Glory of God Ministries
International - (Lilongwe, Malawi)

§

This book written by Dr. Alan Lea is a powerful novel full of insight, understanding, compassion, and tender mercy that will heal hearts that have been broken, wounded and were empty. This book will fill the hearts of many to overflowing.

Father, I thank You for sending this book on the wings of mercy to every person that the enemy has sidelined and imprisoned in darkness, hopelessness, and torment. We thank You that light lives within the words this book contains, breaking off every binding chain.

We thank You for the readers of this book finding themselves empty no more, but alive in the beauty and power of your eternal love.

We thank You for filling their hearts with the wonder of Your plans, purposes, and destinies that You have ordained for them from the foundation of the world. In Jesus' mighty Name. Amen.

James Nesbit

President at Prophetic Art of James Nesbit and Prepare the Way Ministries International - Florence, Alabama, USA

§

I have read this book literally three times through. First, through the eyes of a literary critic (6 stars out of a possible 5). My second trip through was as a pastor and how true it remained to the integrity of Scripture revealed. Again another 6 out of 5.

During the course of my third trip through, I removed the literary critic and pastor's hats and allowed the Holy Spirit to minister to me, the man, from the inside out. I journeyed through the narrative as each of the characters and the takeaway was as powerful, if not more so, than any sermon I have heard or preached myself.

Alain, you knocked it out of the park for sure. It speaks to all demographics and is a must read, especially for our Millennials and our Gen Z (Centennials). I absolutely loved the relevance. Definitely a winner for anyone who will read this book!

Rev. Dr Chris O. Wallas
Church of Christ Ministry – New York (USA)

§

What an awesome story! I am not a big reader, however, to say the least, I was spellbound, and it was difficult to set it down. The way you brought everyone together with all their different issues was amazing. Christian is certainly a strong believer being able to endure the ridicule from his friends, even coming from the background that he did. Then, for him to stand strong in his faith against odds of being rejected by them.

It was certainly awesome for Dominic to finally have the courage to go and talk with the pastor regarding his abuse. It was also wonderful how Christian was able to influence Colton, AJ, Thomas, and Will for Christ.

Although I didn't see the ending coming with Devin being forced to commit murder, it was a relief when Devin couldn't go through with killing his friend. It was a bit disappointing to find that Devin is now having to pay the ultimate price (although understandable). But then this is where this story stops with a promise of being continued. So, I am certainly looking forward to the next volume of this piece of art.

Pastor Alain Lea, thanks again for the opportunity to enjoy this masterpiece. Blessings.

Melvin Burdette

Engineer in Telecommunication, South Carolina (USA)

The Void is one of the best Christian literatures I have ever read, maybe because it perfectly mirrors the gospel of Christ as it really is. The author successfully stands out in this generation by preaching the good news of Christ through a narrative. The author has been able to effectively communicate the love of God to both the saved and unsaved in an overwhelming manner. The use of a colloquial language style as well as the simple present tense in writing this book gives the reader a sense of reality, which makes him feel as though he were a part of the narrative. Also, the characters present in the narrative typify the kind of people one comes across in an average society. My best character in the novel is Christian. I like the fact that his name is his lifestyle. I love the way he was successfully able to preach what Christianity really is, both in words and actions.

Apart from the message of Christ found in the book, I also found the message of "fear-based decisions" and "growth decisions" very insightful. In the sequel to this book, I expect to see if Isaac finds the answers to his questions and becomes a partaker of the life of Christ. If yes, how does his family take it? I would expect to know if Devin had a second chance. I would also like to know what became of Dom's uncle. Did Dom end up telling his mum about the abuse again? What was her reaction? I would also like to know the effect the guys' new-found faith has in their different families. But in this narrative, the author has done a real good job in terms of message and delivery.

Susannah Philips
Writer and Translator (Manchester, UK)

FINAL NOTE

We invite you to continue your experience with *The Void* at our website. Feel free to share how you feel about this novel and read what others are saying, communicate with the author and read our blogs. You can also purchase additional copies of *The Void*.

For more information about booking the author to speak to your organization or group, please contact Christ In All Nations Inc at <u>info@christinallnations.org.</u>

If you enjoyed the message of this book, here are some ideas to help you share this book with others:

∞ Give the book to friends, even strangers, as a gift. They are not just getting a compelling, page-turning thrill ride, but also a magnificent glimpse into the true nature of God that is not often presented in cultures around the globe today.

∞ If you have a website or blog, consider sharing a bit about the book and how it touched your life. Don't give away the plot but recommend that they read it as well.

∞ Write a book review for your local paper, favorite magazine, or website you frequent. Ask your favorite radio show or podcast to invite the author on as a guest. Media people often give more consideration to the requests of their listeners than the press releases of publicists.

∞ If you own a shop, business or you are pastoring a church, consider putting a display of these books on your counter to resell to customers. We make books available at a discounted rate for resale. For individuals, we offer volume discount pricing for orders of five books or more.

∞ Buy a set of books as gifts to battered women's shelters, prisons, rehabilitation homes, and the like where people might be really encouraged by the story and its message.

∞ Talk about the book on e-mail lists you are on, forums you frequent, and other places where you engage other people on the internet. Share how this book impacted your life and offer people the link to the amazon book page.

FOR MORE INFORMATION ABOUT ALAIN LEA AND THE MINISTRY OF CHRIST IN ALL NATIONS, GO TO:
www.christinallnations.org/the-ministry

ABOUT THE AUTHOR

Alain Lea is the author of several books and founder of Christ In All Nations, an international ministry proclaiming the gospel of the triune God. He has been expounding and preaching the untainted grace of our Lord Jesus Christ for more than a decade now.

Alain was born a Cameroonian and raised in a loving family. He suffered great loss when his father died and extreme sickness during most of his childhood. He was miraculously healed by the power of God's Love. He had several encounters with Jesus as a young adult and now enjoys the extravagance of God's astonishing grace with his family in Washington DC, USA.

BOOKS COMING SOON

Heart to Heart (Homologeo)

When the chaos of our daily lives becomes overwhelming, where can we turn for peace and rest? Apostle Alain Lea points to the Source of all hope and strength in *Heart to Heart*, which contains sixty guided prayers.

We all pray . . . some.

We pray to stay sober, centered or solvent. When the lump is deemed malignant, when the money runs out before the month does or when the marriage is falling apart, we pray.

But wouldn't we like to pray more? Better? Stronger? With more fire, faith, and fervency?

Yet we have kids to feed, bills to pay, deadlines to meet. The calendar pounces on our good intentions like a tiger on a rabbit. What about our checkered history with prayer: uncertain words, unmet expectations and unanswered requests?

We are not the first to struggle with prayer. The first followers of Jesus needed prayer guidance too. In fact, prayer is the only tutorial they ever requested and Jesus gave them a prayer, not a lecture on prayer, not the doctrine of prayer; He gave them a quotable, repeatable, portable prayer. Couldn't we use the same?

In *Heart to Heart,* best-selling author Dr. Alain Lea joins readers on a journey to the very heart of Biblical prayer, offering hope for doubts and confidence, even for prayer wimps. Distilling prayers in the Bible down to one pocket-sized prayer, Alain reminds readers that prayer is not a privilege for the pious nor the art of a chosen few. Prayer is simply a heartfelt conversation between God and his child. Let the conversation begin…

Overcoming Fear

It is reported now, more than ever, that many people struggle with feelings of depression and stress that are fueled by fear. Alain Lea's new book, *Overcoming Fear*, provides a candid and revealing look into how fear works and how to be free from it forever. Once fear is removed, you are free to live the life God has designed for you.

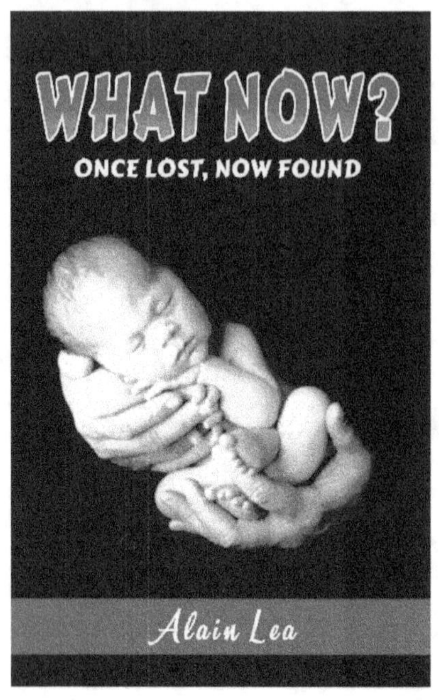

What Now?
Once Lost Now Saved

It is so easy to forget what faith is all about. We struggle so much, work so hard, and fail so often that we frequently sense something in the equation of life must be missing.

Alain Lea argues that what we are missing is the gospel in a fuller, more powerful understanding of Jesus and what His finished work means for everyday life.

During his adolescence, Alain Lea discovered the power of the gospel in his own life by experiencing encounters with Jesus. He shares in this book what He learned when Jesus became more real to him. Lea delves deeply into the fundamentals of faith, explaining the implications of Christ's sufficiency as the revelation that sets us free and keeps us anchored through life's storms.

Ultimately, Alain reminds us that Jesus is the whole of the equation as he boldly proclaims that humanity was once lost and now found in Christ Jesus.